THE
FIFTH
HORSEMAN

Lauran Paine

has written over 900 books under his own name and various pseudonyms. Born in Duluth, Minnesota, he is a descendant of the Revolutionary War patriot and author, Thomas Paine. He moved with his family to California at a young age, and his subsequent experience in many facets of Western life, including the livestock trade and rodeos, would form the foundation of respect for the ways of the Old West as seen through the eyes of the very early settlers. Paine served in the United States Navy during World War Two and began writing for Western pulp magazines following his discharge. His Western fiction is characterized by strong plots, authentic details and an apparently effortless ability to construct situation and character.

THE
FIFTH
HORSEMAN

Lauran Paine

ROUNDUP LARGE PRINT
HAMPTON, NEW HAMPSHIRE

Library of Congress Cataloging-in-Publication Data

Paine, Lauran.
    The fifth horseman / Lauran Paine.
        p. (large print) cm.
    ISBN 0-7927-1857-7. -- ISBN 0-7927-1856-9 (softcover)
    1. Large type books.   I. Title.
    [PS3566.A34F5   1994]
    813' .54--dc20   93-30321
                                                              CIP

Published in Large Print by arrangement with the
Golden West Literary Agency by Roundup Large Print,
an imprint of Chivers North America, 1 Lafayette Road,
Hampton, NH 03842-0015.

Printed in the United States of America

CHAPTER ONE

The land flowed in a lonely way to the dim merging of heaven and earth. A lonely land, scarcely inhabited except by dimly seen riders hurrying through. A great lift and fall of land spreading out interminably like water frozen in motion, mottled with blue sage, scrub-oak clumps and new grass, for it was Spring, and overhead wild geese passed in miraculously formed triangles, their lonely screams coming down to the men below. To the Old Man, all gaunt and iron-like, standing between his big sons, Carl and Matthew. And behind them, leaning against the ugly stone house, were their rifles.

They were of a size, the three of them, except that Carl and Matthew were less gaunt, more round and massively powerful than the Old Man was. And in the face they were different, too. The Old Man's features were like agate; old, veined agate, bruised and pounded by long, suffering years, by the high winds of strife and the low moments of softness, brief enough in his life.

And their eyes were different for passion smouldered in Matthew's gaze. A strong and

1

lusty passion for life, for love, for hate, deep as the wells of hell. Carl's eyes, back-ringed, were still subdued, and in their depths lay a power of gentleness, a haunted thoughtfulness none of the others possessed.

But in all else they were the same. In their rough clothing, high-topped, flat-heeled boots, the dark shell-belts and holstered guns, in the big fists, calloused, swollen from labour, in the way they stood, better than six feet, strong as bulls, wide-legged and waiting, watching the curl of dust rise higher as horsemen approached.

Carl reached out to finger a little slip of a tree close at hand It was an unconscious, nervous gesture and the Old Man saw it as such from the corner of his deep-set eyes.

"You scairt, boy?" he asked in his harsh way. "If you are, go take your rifle around the side of the house."

"I ain't scairt," Carl said, and bitterness crept into his voice. "This tree's dying. They said Oklahoma was a rich land. Things'd prosper here."

"And they lied," the Old Man rumbled. "They lied. I told you a dozen times our family's made for struggle and hardship. That there ain't a thing in this life we'll get without it. If the tree dies it's because it ain't strong— ain't willing to fight for survival."

2

"I get sick of fighting," Carl said. "I get sick of being—"

"Then you're weak!"

"I'm *not* weak! I just want to live without fighting all the time. Without taking what ain't mine, without being hated. I want to get me a family and maybe farm a piece of land. Plant things, watch them grow."

"They're getting closer," Matthew said, for it was always Matthew who saw the Old Man's side, who came between Carl and their father, who understood them both in their different ways, who had always wondered which was right—or even if they weren't *both* right. Such a thing could be.

The Old Man's sunken eyes shone like wet stone. They moved a little to gauge the distance of the horsemen, their numbers, their angling course towards the stone house, built like a fort and just as ugly, just as forbidding. But when he spoke it wasn't about the posse, for his mind was still cluttered with fragments of words, sharp, like broken crockery.

"Man's born of the soil, Carl. He's put here to suffer and if he ain't a fighting man he don't last. You got to give as hard as you get—harder. You got to fight; you got to take what you been denied. Who are you to deserve better?"

Matthew interrupted. "That's Harry

3

Cumberland in the lead," he said. "I recognize his horse."

The Old Man fell silent. At his side, big gnarled fists hung, all knotted and tensed. "Preacher Harry," he said, with wonderful scorn. "The preacher with a hang-rope on his saddle."

The riders swept up, slowed, grew silent as they approached the three big men and finally drew rein, halted altogether. Five of them, rough looking, weathered, in coarse wool shirts and stained trousers that were tucked into their boots. Their hats were wide-brimmed and they were armed with pistols, rifles and knives. Their leader was a spindly-shanked man, raffish and venomous-appearing, with eyes as black as sin, looking down.

"Jacob Fenwick—you was warned."

The Old Man and his sons were silent, as still as the night and stalwart.

"There's witnesses say they saw the lot of you run off a hundred head of four-year-olds from Parson's place north of Osage."

"Then they lie," the Old Man said. "We been right here."

"I ain't here to argue."

"I know that," the Old Man said sharply. "I know why you're here, Preacher. You and your rope. Well, I got no great fear of dying, but by Christ, it won't be you or your rope'll do the job and I'm telling you *that!*"

"You been warned," Cumberland repeated, watching the three of them from his saddle.

"So I have been," the Old Man boomed. "Now I'm going to do a mite of warning of my own. 'I ever catch you or them others with you on this side of the range again, making trouble, I won't use no rope, Preacher—no rope. And you remember that."

"Folks around the settlement have about had enough, Jacob. The Lord's on our side."

"Maybe he is and maybe he ain't. One thing's certain," the Old Man said. "If He'll stay neutral—stand off a mite—he's going to see the damndest fight He ever did see, one of these days, if you and them others don't leave us in peace."

"There're witnesses against you."

"Liars. A pack of settlement liars. My boys and me been right here on our own land for a week steady."

"You got proof of that?" Cumberland asked.

"Proof? Sure; my word—the word of Matthew and Carl—only that wouldn't be good enough for you and yours, so I got no proof, have I?"

Cumberland moved in the saddle, looked at his companions, who were staring down at the three big men. It made the Old Man smile in

5

his wintery way, how Preacher Harry looked to his allies for support in what would happen if any of them made a bad move.

In tones of acid, the Old Man said: "Make a prayer, Preacher. Maybe that'll stiffen your spine enough for you to start something. You'll need more'n stiffening the first fault you make. Don't look to *them*—you're out front, *they* ain't. Say a prayer and maybe we'll miss you with the first shots."

Cumberland's dark eyes burned. "We come here to see proof or otherwise," he said. "There's witnesses—"

"You said that before and I told you they're liars, whoever they are." The Old Man raised his left arm, thrust it out. "See yonder? *That's* what we been doing this past week. If you can work up the ground like that in less than a week I'd like to see you do it."

The riders turned, gazed steadily at the rich earth, brown and gently steaming in the warm Spring sun, freshly ploughed and broken up for seeding. Maybe eighty acres of it.

The Old Man's arm fell back to his side and several of the men behind Harry Cumberland crossed their hands upon their saddlehorns and sat relaxed, waiting for this to be over with.

Preacher Harry was a long time speaking. It was as though he were wrestling inwardly with something. Then he said, "You could have done that at night, maybe."

"What?" the Old Man retorted. "Plough by moonlight? You're dumber'n I thought you were. It's easy to see you never held a plough in your life."

"Not plough—run off them four-year-olds."

"That's crazier yet. 'You ever try to drive four-year-olds Texas cattle in the dark?"

One of the possemen cleared his throat and spat amber liquid, shot Harry Cumberland a long look and lifted his reins. The others followed his example. They all wheeled and rode westerly in a thin spiral of dust. Preacher Harry's eyes were black agate, his mouth below a red face, bloodless and sucked flat until the lips were hidden. He went after the others with a fury in his heart that was stifling, a humiliation he would never forget.

Jacob didn't move until the men from Osage were small, skittering spots on the daylight, far out, and although he had won, had belittled Cumberland before others, there was no triumph in his face.

"Let's get back to work," he said, turning away with contempt in every angular line of him.

Matthew lingered, watching the fading shapes. His lips were sardonically twisted, his

7

bright, hot eyes laughing without mirth.

Carl walked away and there was flecked spit of a sour kind in his gullet. He went towards the barn with it in his mouth.

The days spun on, the sun got warmer, the sky held its fleecy clouds until the warmth turned to heat and the great orb over everything became lemon-yellow and glittering and summer was everywhere.

And the Fenwicks harvested their hay crop, finished working their cattle, truckled through the myriad chores which had built up through the brutal cold winter against the time when men could work out of doors again. Came at last to a time of pause every countryman knows with the changing of seasons, like he's standing with his head a little to one side, listening.

Busied themselves divergently, Carl, working with his hands. He was good at mending harness, saddles, at creating things. He had a way with him, too, for planting, so the Old Man had used him for the sewing and it had been a bountiful crop. Carl, talked to the sky when he planted and after the green appeared low and velvety along the ground, there would be a hunger in his eyes. A yearning to see things grow out of him. For life and usefulness to spring from his hands.

But when he was near the Old Man, there

8

was an emptiness in his face.

Matthew broke colts to saddle and tasted the wine of his own blood. There was a wild grace to Matthew, a suppleness rarely found in big men. And he smiled at things. Mostly at secret things only he knew about; like dreams he'd had, or memories. Also of times he'd met Judith Anne along the creeks or out where the salt-licks were.

He rarely laughed aloud, but he'd smile and of them all, Matthew was the best with animals. Old Jacob was too tempered for breaking colts and Carl shrank from the cruelty. You couldn't break colts without cruelty; only generations yet to come would believe that you could. In 1871, Oklahoma folks knew you couldn't and they were right.

Just like Jacob had been right when he'd said the Fenwicks hadn't stolen Will Parson's four-year-olds. Just like he'd been right when he'd said a man must fight to survive.

It was like Jacob to speak bluntly, even hurtingly, to those around him. There were dark seeds in his mind and always had been. He was a strange and cruel man. He believed simply in survival. Asked no odds, had a god in his mind who was sharp-limned yet obscure. Jacob knew this god's mind, because it was his own mind. His preachments were Jacob's preachments. But he had never been

9

able to dissemble—to picture the face, the eyes, the details of this god. In late years, he had striven hard, too, but the phantom remained a shadow. It troubled him and often he would mutter to himself about it. The more he thought on it, the stranger he became to others.

He believed as he had said, implicitly and without reservations. He had raised his sons in that manner. " . . . Our family's made for struggle and hardship. There ain't a thing in life we'll get without it . . . Man's born of the soil. He's put here to suffer and if he ain't a fighting man, he don't last . . . You got to take what you been denied . . . " He raised his sons in that image. He had raised a third son to fifteen years of age believing that, but he was dead now. Dead of colic in the depth of winter and you could hear the slop of water in him when he tried to breathe. That had been Luke, with eyes as blue as sunflowers and hair that was a mane of untamed gold.

The settlement folk stayed clear of Fenwicks. Like the Indians who lingered in the land, who killed by stealth, a Fenwick was something to fear, to watch, to shun, and when rustlers rode with the hot dust of yellow earth twisting to life along their backtrails, it was said the Old Man led his sons. And it was known that, until now, when Matthew and

10

Carl had come to manhood with minds of their own, to call out one, was to call all three out.

How did they survive 'way out there by themselves, alone and apart, unless they were in league with the night-riders, the redskins, all manner of devils? And again, they were all lightning-quick with guns, deadly as Old Scratch himself, at a hundred yards or closer. That was common knowledge, too, so when people rode out to talk they went in numbers like Harry Cumberland had done, for the Fenwicks were a scourge, a dread and a terror, 'way out there in their ugly stone house, and the Old Man's wife, whom few had ever seen, who rarely spoke and never went to the settlement, and whose spirit if she'd ever had one, had long since succumbed to Jacob's force, even she was more legend than person, to the folk of Osage.

The 'Nations had its share and more, of renegades, outlaws, bandits of every stripe and shade, but most kept moving, or died, or were hung, or just plain faded away. Not the Fenwicks. They had been in that stone house as long as anyone knew, for this land was fresh and new itself, and whenever a crime was committed it had to be those strange, harsh people. Suspecting them had become local custom, fetish, as natural as putting little

11

sacks of asafoetida in water-troughs to cleanse saddle, stock of catarrh in the Spring.

There was a mote of truth in it, too. Old Jacob *had* moon-lighted cattle. And even if he hadn't done it, his appearance, the way he lived and talked and raised his sons would have made it appear that he did, for he believed foremost in survival. "Take what's been denied you . . . "

Southerly, three miles, was the Parkinson place. John Parkinson was a frog of a man. he teetered when he walked because his legs were pipe-stems, while his torso was immensely wide and deep, incredibly powerful. A-horseback, he was like a giant or a centaur. He was swarthy—from a raping fifty years before—and as moody as any Indian. As wild in anger, as totally oblivious to danger any time, but when drunk, he was a devil. His brain was small and tight. Thoughts came ponderously and thinking was pain. But he had courage and loyalty.

His wife had perished from rattler-bite when Judith Anne was thirteen and Ellie was eleven. That had been in '65, when the war ended. Since then, John had run his scrubby cattle on the same range Jacob Fenwick ran his. In co-operation, there was strength, for John's daughters rode and kept the house, after a fashion; there were three Parkinsons to

12

watch the stock and three Fenwicks.

Ellie Parkinson was the best at minding the house, because Judith Anne, dark like her father, alive and bursting with energy so that she seemed to be moving, even when she was sitting still, lived on a horse. Judith Anne was pretty. High-breasted, about the size of young oranges, and long-legged, wasp-waisted, with a world of glittery black hair, that flew in the wind and when she rode Comanche style— astride; her head would be thrust forward, full lips parted and dark blood staining in under her cheeks.

Ellie was quieter, with deep fire. Mostly it was hidden, but you could see it from time to time when Ellie was aroused. But she moved slower than Judith Anne, thought more and spoke less. Occasionally an odd abstraction would mask her face, making it stoic, unhandsome, like an Indian's face.

And Ellie was shorter than Judith Anne, although they weighed the same. With Ellie, it was pushed around more, so that Ellie had curves in places where most of the settlement girls didn't even have places.

The Parkinsons were mistrusted also; thought darkly of, like the Fenwicks were. If any distinction was made between them, it was to say Old Jacob had wild white-man courage, where John Parkinson had wild

13

Indian courage, for no one, not even Preacher Harry Cumberland, would deny that it required courage—or—insanity—to stay ten miles out, when redskins and renegades were rampant and hardly a night passed someone wasn't hacked to death in their bed or gut-shot when they went out to chore the critters in the dawn.

That was why the settlement folk around Osage suspected the worst and made no secret of the fact that they did so, whenever they encountered the Old Man or one of his sons, providing they were in force. When they happened to meet all of them together, Fenwicks and Parkinsons, regardless of the odds, they said nothing. Three Fenwicks and John Parkinson were enough at one sight, all together, to make God himself say hush.

But craggy Will Parson was in no mood to be cautious when he found himself shy a hundred grassed-out four-year-olds, either, for with the money from them, he'd meant to hitch up and leave Oklahoma. Take his family where civilisation wasn't so long catching up to folks.

The harder he tried to find out what had become of his animals, who had run them off, the easier it became for him to believe the Fenwicks had done it. There were dozens of mean people who would say they'd seen riders; recognised the *three* of them. The will to injure, to cause trouble, that came out of in-bred, hateful small minds, made it sound convincing enough. Preacher Harry told Will Parson he *knew* . . . just plain *knew* . . .

"You seen them, Harry?"

"In my second sight, Will, as plain as day. The Old Man—Matthew and Carl, as plain as day. Me'n a few others went out there, too, but the Old Man denied it and the Lord told me to come away."

"He should have told you to hang them. Them and Parkinson, too." Parson looked at his hands and thought of Jacob and John Parkinson; thought of Judith Anne and got hot behind his belt and closed his hands into knots of hard gristle, felt ashamed, too, and left Harry Cumberland alone. Rode home with his black thoughts of hanging, and of other things.

Will Parson was a talker, a threatener, a man to clench up his fist and shake it and swear almighty oaths, and when he spoke of the thing which became an obsession with him—the stolen four-year-olds—he would get as dark in the face as thunder. When he was found murdered in the pearl-grey dawn, the settlement was appalled; stunned into silence.

There was nothing to indicate who had

15

knifed Will Parson. There were no tracks in the summer-dry ground, no shod-horse marks, like a white man would make, no moccasin sign of a redskin. No sign of any kind, but it didn't matter, for the ones Will had spoken out against the hardest were naturally blamed. Behind the hand at first, later they were openly accused of his murder. But all anyone knew—ever *did* know for that matter—was that Will Parson had been stabbed under the ribs, the knife twisted round and sideways and he had died in the lead-grey dawn, with his own claret softening the earth where he'd threshed and bleated and finally become still.

The talk was still rife when someone took a wild shot at Preacher Harry, one night when he was returning home from a call on Widow Harris. Some of the cowboys snickered over that, because Widow Harris was an obliging little woman. They said some brush-popper had been angry because it took Preacher Harry so danged long in there. But Cumberland said he'd recognised the men. There had been *three* of them . . . that was all he'd said. There had been three of them.

The snickers died away and anger, suspicion, fear, came fiercely in its place. Those Fenwicks again. 'Y Christ, a man's life wasn't safe even in the settlement, with them sneaking around shooting everyone who talked against them. The timid became furtive and the bold became inflamed. Before long there wasn't a crime in Indian Territory that didn't have witnesses who'd seen three big shadows loping away afterwards. And, of course, the Fenwicks, ten miles out, alone and apart, across land rare few men dared travel by day and none by night, were the last to know.

So Matthew met Judith Anne by the breaks that lined the bottoms along Chagrin Creek— called Shag-grin Crick—and looked into the black, soiled water without feeling any cooler for all the shade of the willows, and suspected nothing. Had no inkling that black wings were rustling and the sifting sand was running out.

Knew only that Judith Anne was there smelling of burnt copper and crushed sage. That her eyes as black as burnt bones, but ten times as shiny, were there. And that her long legs, drawn up, hugged close by round golden arms, were flattening her small breasts. Knew only those things—and a hotness.

He didn't speak and neither did she. It was as though the dark, turgid waters mesmerised them both. Sweat ran down Matthew's cheek and fell against the earth, got sucked under, Judith Anne hugged herself tighter and looked at Matthew's bigness, all sprawling and relaxed.

17

"Paw got a bear off the east range. He says there was sign it'd killed cattle back in there."

It always started out like that when they were together, alone. Casual, neighbourly, indifferent, like they were brother and sister. It was part of their game, and even the impatience that led them to ride their horses so hard to get there was forgotten while they acted out their game, lingered over words that were goads, made delicious torture of the waiting.

Matthew ran a hand through his heavy thatch of auburn hair and gazed with wonderful simplicity at her. "There's more'n bears back there." The singleness of his want showed clear and hungry. "It's all right for your Paw, but *you'd* better not go back in there. More renegades back there'n you can shake a stick at. If they got their hands on you, you'd *never* get back." Visualising what would happen to her made the big vein in his throat swell and ebb gustily.

"Paw met some settlement men a few days back. He says they got their backs up about something."

"Indians. They're always worrying about Indians. As close as they stay to Osage, you'd think there wasn't anything in the out-country, *but* Indians."

"I wonder what it's like, living in the settlement." Her dark eyes grew still with thought and, for a moment, the other thing which had been in them, was pushed aside.

"Just figure what it'd be like if there was a hundred of you and a hundred of me, then you'll know."

She laughed. "I don't think they'd get much work done, if they were that close all the time . . . A hundred you's and a hundred me's."

He knew the game was over, so he straightened up off the ground and reached for her. Felt the dull pound of her heart and the whisper of her breath. Kissed her, closed big hands over her and let the roar in his head run free.

When she was gazing up at him she said, "Matt; if we ever get caught, your paw'd kill us."

"He won't. By now I got things worked out so I know when to come here."

"What if we get in trouble—what then?"

"Can't get in trouble. You just keep watching the curve of the moon like the squaws do. They know."

She twisted her full lips up into a lazy smile. "The cane breaks got our secret."

He nodded without commenting. Lately this had come more and more to obsess him,

19

this late awakening, these meetings and how he contrived to hoodwink his brother and the Old Man. There was less satisfaction in the deception by far, than there was lying there with Judith Anne—by far.

Sweat was running under his shirt. He sucked in a big gulp of air and listened to the thump of his heart. She could do this to him. Get him all afire in a sweaty moment.

"What if I never came back?"

He smiled into her teasing eyes. "You'll come back; you got the hunger just as strong as I have."

"How do you know?"

"Lots of ways. You're human same as me. Sometimes I think you got it worse'n I have. Sometimes you act like you have, anyway."

"I don't say I haven't," she said, her gaze withdrawing from him a little. "Sometimes I ride over here even when I know you won't be here."

He watched the shadows deep in her eyes. Saw how her heavy mouth hung open after she stopped speaking, the tightness of her skin; how the sun, hot and yellow, touched her arms, neck, and shoulders, turned them copper-gold colour. Then he leaned back on the grass and looked straight upwards, deliciously tired and spent.

"I hope this goes on forever, Judith Anne."

"Why shouldn't it?"

"I don't know. I got to feeling sometimes like it won't; like something'll come along and spoil it. Like maybe you'll take a notion it's wrong."

"If I was going to think that, Matt, it would've been after the first time we met here."

"Maybe you'll get over it, some way."

"No," she said quickly, "won't either of us get over it. I won't and I know you won't."

"How can you tell?" he asked, twisting his head to gaze at her. "*I* know I won't, but how could you know?"

She touched her blouse with one hand. "In here. I got the secret of that kind of knowing in here."

"It's a good secret, Judith Anne. Maybe later on we could get married even."

"What would we live on," she said, "your paw'd kick you out sure if we did that."

"We'd live by cattle, like everyone else does."

"Where'd we get the cattle? Where'd the money come from for that.?"

He looked at her for a moment in silence. "I reckon a rope's as good as Yankee dollars," he said. "When you ain't got the one, you use the other."

He plucked a blade of grass, twisted it in his

21

fingers. "It'd be sort of nice being married, wouldn't it?"

Her black stare became restless, liquid-soft and sheathed looking, like new velvet. "I guess so, only what I've seen of being married . . . " It trailed off. She touched the hand he was twisting the grass stem with and her fingers were moist. "One thing about it; I'd make you want to throw stones at those settlement girls. Make you want to stomp them in the dust."

"You've already made me want to do that," he said, bending over her, tracing out the wilful curvature of her mouth, the faint lilt at the outer corners of her eyes and the high bridge of her nose where a tiny spray of girlhood-freckles still showed.

"You've already made me want to do that and I've never been around the settlement girls."

She half smiled at a sudden thought. "Do you think Carl and Ellie are meeting like we do?"

"Carl?" His surprise turned to a grim. "Naw; I can't see Carl down in the breaks. For that matter, I can't see Ellie here, either. They're different."

"Don't be fooled," Judith Anne said. "Ellie'd go. She'd go with *you*, if she had a chance. I know my sister. She may act quiet

22

and all, but I know what goes on inside her. Carl ought to meet her once. I'd bet on what'd happen, Matt. Besides, there's more to Ellie than there is to me."

"Different," Matthew mumbled. "She hardly ever talks and I don't think I've seen her ride out this last year at all."

Judith Anne's glance became sharp and scheming. "I'll send Ellie to the salt-lick near Big Bend tomorrow, and you send Carl. Let's see what happens. 'Want to?"

"All right," he said, not very interested and disliking the idea in more ways than one. It was something close to betrayal in his mind.

"Look at the sun; I got to get back."

She squirmed upwards, straightened her clothes and stood as straight as an arrow. There was impish delight in her expression. "Don't you forget to send Carl."

"You're sure set on it, aren't you?"

"Well," she said, "it'll be interesting to watch, won't it?"

He got up and brushed himself off; didn't look at her. "Why get them all tangled up?" When he glanced around, she was staring at him with a dusky darkness, her mouth pulled in a little. "All right," he said, "I'll send him."

She kissed him and left, riding like an Indian, great wealth of black hair flying, body moving with perfect grace, unconscious tim-

23

ing. He recalled the strange vitalness in her face when she looked down at him from the saddle. The hawk-like intensity of her glance and the singing richness of her closed mouth. He groaned aloud.

Why had he let her talk him into sending his brother to the salt-lick, anyway? he tugged up the cincha, toed in and sprang upon his horse, thinking that Judith Anne was dangerous some way. Really dangerous; and it worried him, for he knew she had more than just a woman's hold on a man. She was in his blood, in his mind eroding away the things his disillusioned mother had only hinted darkly at. Bad things, unclean, sinful, poisonous even, and ungodly.

How did she make him so aware of danger? No colt ever had no matter how wild, how spoilt or vicious. No man or storm, no war-party of redskins.

He wasn't sure, exactly, what Judith Anne *did* to him, he only knew it was there, inside him, like a swollen seed of some kind from which was growing a big, strangling vine.

She had planted the thing, watered it, scratched up the pink wetness of his inner self to nourish it, and it wasn't a clean or rightful thing, and although he hungered, hurt and grew hot and restless inside when he thought of Judith Anne, some poison out of her was drowning him inside.

What? The need? Yes; partly that—mostly that, probably, but it was more too, and that was what he tried to define and couldn't.

He rode all the way back home reaching up in his mind, straining to grasp it, bring it down into the light of reason and examine it—and couldn't. It never settled down, always eluded him. He balled up his fist and struck the saddlehorn until his hand hurt, then he relaxed and rode along with a strange urgency in his face that he wasn't aware of and that his family didn't see because it was gone by the time he put the horse up and trudged across the yard to the ugly stone house.

The Old Man looked at him only once from beneath shaggy brows and said nothing. He missed seeing the wild strangeness in his father's brief stare. His mother flung him a questioning look and motioned towards the plank table where food lay. Carl seemed strained and slower than usual in speech, as though sharing Matthew's gloominess.

"We're going to move the cattle tomorrow," he said, when Matthew was eating, head low, lamplight giving his auburn hair a red-burnished look. Carl went on: "Paw rode the breaks today. There's enough browse down there to last till Fall."

Matthew's spoon hung in mid-air. His

25

stomach drew into a hard ball and very slowly he sought his father's face. Sickness gushed deep down, flooding him. And shame, because it was there as plain as day in the Old Man's eyes. He had seen them!

Matthew pushed back the bowl. "I got to look at the horses," he said, and left the house. Walked through the faint light of night, white and eerie, spurs ringing, face almost as pale as the moonwash and his eyes clear and bitter, like new ice.

He stood by the corral looking at nothing; at the night, which was power and hush and greatness, with its swollen moon worn shapeless from bearing litters of stars, and thought of Judith Anne. That she wouldn't care in the least that the Old Man had seen them. Imagined how her bold black eyes would narrow with scorn, knowing as she did how the Old Man thought about things like that; about girls and men and that you married them afterwards.

"Matthew?"

Carl's shadow loomed up heavy, big as a bear, rolling as it approached. "Over here," Matthew said.

Carl stopped, leaned upon the corral stringers. "Nice night," he said."

"Real nice."

Without moving his head, Carl cast a

sidling glance. "What's troubling you?"

"Nothing; why do you ask?"

"There was something back there in the house. 'You and the Old Man fighting?"

"No. Not yet anyway, but I got a notion we will be."

Carl looked at the ground for a while without speaking, then he said, "I want to leave here, Matthew. I want to go somewhere else."

"I know . . . "

"And have a place of my own." Carl was looking straight ahead with his dark-ringed eyes as sombre, as still as death. "A family, some crop-land, neighbours. 'Not fighting all the time . . . hating. Having folks shy off from me."

Knowing what was behind his brother's words, Matthew said, "Mostly, the Old Man knows what's right, Carl."

"Well—no one's ever always wrong . . . But the fighting, hating everyone . . . being hated."

"He's right about struggle and strife, Carl. We'll always have that. All of us will. You can't run away from life. That's what it is, really; life."

"I don't believe it."

"I do. I *know* it. I got reason to know. Fighting ain't just done with guns, either. 'Man's got to struggle. He's got to watch some-

27

thing doesn't catch him up, make a settlement man out of him."

"What's wrong with that?" Carl said in a rising tone. "That's what I *want*. Neighbours, friends, a family . . ."

There was that difference between them, Matthew thought, so he stopped speaking. There was so much between them that was different.

"Well," he said after a while, "don't get worked up. Things'll work out. It don't matter a whole lot."

"It does to me. I want to leave the Territory."

"All right. Did you see the Old Man when he came back from riding the breaks today?"

"Yes, I was here."

"Did he say anything?"

"No; just put up his horse, went over by the well and sat there like a stone, like he does sometimes. Sat there till close to suppertime."

Matthew balled up his fists until the nails left imprints in his palms. "Ellie's going to check cattle at the Big Bend salt-lick tomorrow," he said in a halting tone.

"Big Bend?"

"Yeah."

"John's got no sense, sending a girl alone like that."

Matthew squinted at the tiniest of stars.

28

"There's enough Indian in all of 'em to smell trouble a mile off."

"Not a girl."

"Maybe not. If I didn't have to put new washers in the wagon tomorrow I'd sort of ride out and see she was all right."

Carl looked at his brother in a still and questioning way. "What're you going to fix the wagon for?"

"The Old Man said something about going to Osage for flour and cornmeal a few days back."

"Tomorrow? You know what he's said about that. We all go or none of us go."

"He didn't say tomorrow. Anyway, if you're not here we just won't go, that's all. I figured you might look after Ellie tomorrow."

"All right," Carl said, scowling. "Will he get mad if I'm not here and he means to go tomorrow?"

"Naw; what good would it do him?"

Carl moved off. "John ought to be switched," he mumbled.

Watching his brother fade into shadows, Matthew wondered why he was doing it. He didn't want Carl down in the breaks with Ellie. Judith Anne did, though. That was why he was doing it. Because Judith Anne wanted it, like she didn't want to get married. It made him feel mean and treacherous. Judith Anne

29

wanted to make Carl and Ellie slaves like she and Matthew were slaves. By God, *that's* what it was; what he'd tried to define on the ride back. Judith Anne wanted her sister and his brother to lose their freedom like Matthew had lost his.

"Carl . . . ?"

His brother turned, over by the well. Softly his words floated back to Matthew. "The Old Man's coming," he said in a warning way.

Matthew peered squarely towards the stone house. It was hard to make out the rusty figure at first, tall and gaunt and forging through the night with a thrusting tread, meeting the night like he met everything else—head-on.

He saw Carl start out towards the grain field. There'd never been a closeness between his father and brother.

The Old Man stopped in front of Matthew without speaking. There was a shadowed cragginess to his seamed face and where his eyes lay deep were blacker shadows. "Well," the Old Man said, "what have you got to say?"

"Nothing."

"Nothing," the Old Man spat out. "Nothing but sin and wickedness!"

Matthew thought: *It was denied me so I took it and you taught me that yourself!*

"What kind of a man are you?"

There was no argument to make for a hot

30

reply drove the Old Man into a frenzy. Saliva grew sticky at the edges of his mouth when he got roiled. Matthew remained still and quiet.

"I seen the two of you in the grass, wallowing around like a couple of cub bears."

Matthew burnt with shame, with terrible embarrassment, because he knew the Old Man was hawk-eyed, never missed a shading, a detail, a track or sign of any kind.

"You got a course to take, Matthew. You got to take it." And the Old Man walked away, all stiff and awkward and unlike himself, with the soft night splotching him with filigreed shadows.

CHAPTER TWO

Carl rode the ridges like he'd been taught to do since childhood. It was better to be seen and *see*, than to be seen and *not* see. An arrow was silent, an ambush fatal.

He rode without fear, but with watchfulness, for this was his environment; his life since earliest times. Rode through the morning quiet with only his hat for cover; with the burning sun on him, and his horse's hooves raising dust in transparent streamers.

There was a sullen glow over the range, a

sallowness, hurting to the eye, a painful glare which quivered like jelly when he strained to see far ahead where glassy water, dark and sullen and greasy looking, made a big hook; a Big Bend.

When he finally saw her though, she wasn't riding towards the salt-lick at all, but towards the shaded cane breaks. Towards the creek bottom where coolness lay, thick enough to bend. He angled so as to intercept her and there was nothing in his mind but condemnation for John Parkinson, for no matter how coyote a girl was, it was wicked to make her ride alone in such country, in such weather.

When he came up, Ellie was standing beside her horse watching his approach. He knew she had heard him long before, but her erectness hadn't lessened any and even though he was positive she'd recognised him, the little pistol was in her hand. When she spoke his name, it squirted out of her mouth, sharp sounding.

He swung off.

There was a dapple of sweat on her forehead, her upperlip, and the darkness of her gaze was wide, all-seeing. She seemed scarcely to be breathing. The fullness of her blouse, jutting and heavy, was stilled.

"You put a scare into me."

"I expect I did," he said, listening to her

horse sucking water around the mouthpiece of its bit. "You bound for the salt-lick?"

"Yes. I was headed there, but this shade looked so all-fired good I just had to come down here for a little breather."

"Feels cooler down here all right," he mumbled, and looped his reins around a willow, pushed back his hat and felt drying sweat under the shirt, cooling his flesh.

"What're you doing down here; looking for stock?"

"Just looking," he said.

She glanced at her drinking horse, moved awkwardly at the very edge of the creek where the soil was spongy. Looked farther away, across the creek, at nothing, and colour mounted under her skin. She tightened her grasp on the split reins unconsciously. Hc was watching her in a mild and unblinking way.

"Ellie," he said quiet simply, "you're sure pretty standing there like that."

"Shame," she said and gave the horse's reins a yank.

"It's nothing to be ashamed of. You really are."

"You hadn't ought to tell me that, Carl."

"Maybe I hadn't," he said, "but it's true." He went closer, took the reins from her and looped them so the horse was back in the

33

shadows like his horse was. "You got a little-time," he said. "Walk with me along the creek."

She looked up without speaking. There was nothing in Carl Fenwick's face to trouble a girl; there never had been and she'd sought it often, so they walked, twisting through the rank growth of willows, following the creek and the lean shade along its bank, and under the straining coarse cloth of her blouse, the heart beat solidly, for a girl knew things like an animal knew them; by instinct, and Ellie was like that. Like an animal. All quiet and wary and willing. All still inside and tremulous.

"I'd like to tell you how it is with me, Ellie," he said when they stopped in a tiny clearing where clumps of creek-grass grew like toadstools, like shaggy hummocks. The black watchfulness of her glance, the utter stillness of her face troubled him when he looked down though, and he turned to go on.

"Carl."

He faced back from ten feet away and she made no move to move after him. "Yes?"

"I'll listen."

"Naw; I guess not. It'll sound foolish, Ellie. Anyway, it's more'n likely wrong. Even Matt thinks that."

"Then *I'll tell you* something," she said. "I

34

think of the Fenwicks you're least likely to be wrong."

He blinked at her uneasily.

She sat on one of the grass hummocks and he tried not to notice how her skirt was tight-drawn around the curve of hip, the sturdy roundness of her leg. "You think," she said quietly, without looking up at him. "Matt and your paw don't."

"Why, yes, they do, Ellie. We just think different is all. The Old Man's a fighter. Been fighting all his life. And Matt . . . He fights, too, but he's got more things to fight, some way. I can feel it. A lot of Matthew's fights are inside him." He watched her profile. It was stoically unchanged and unchanging. "You don't understand me, do you?"

"He don't put up much of a fight," she said acidly, and he went back and dropped down near her, perplexed appearing. "Matthew's a man-fighter, that's all. Just a man-fighter."

"I expect I'm the one doesn't understand now, Ellie," Carl said.

"Don't you? Judith Anne's got a rope around Matthew, a foot thick. He won't fight it and he can't break it. That's what I mean."

"Judith Anne? He likes her, sure. Why shouldn't he?"

"No reason," Ellie said, turning her head so she could see his damp face in the drawn out

35

willow shadows. "All I'm saying is that Matthew can't get free of her. Maybe you don't know as much about it as I do. I reckon you don't. You don't look like you do. Matthew don't tell you things, does he?"

"He don't talk about Judith Anne, no," Carl said.

"Just as well . . . " The words died, their echoes dwindled and she sat there looking at him for a moment before she spoke again, without the same vibrancy to her voice. "What were you going to tell me, Carl?"

"Nothing," he said, because there was something hard and unpleasant in the glad with them now; there was no longer any mellowness, any softness where he might imprint with words the feelings he had.

She bent forward, touched his bare neck with her fingers. "I want to hear it. I want you to tell me, Carl."

At her touch, new sweat burst out between his shoulders. "I wish I could," he said, "only you'll act like Matthew acts. Like the Old Man'd act if I was to tell him."

"No I won't. Try me."

The fingers worked his damp flesh idly, kneading it like dough until he had to move out of her reach and her hand fell back to her side.

"Well—I want to leave, Ellie, that's all."

36

He looked at her face, there was no change in it. She remained impassive, dark eyes still and bottomless. The wide swell of her mouth closed without pressure, heavy and dark.

"Go on," she said.

"Get some land somewhere and grow things. Make an orchard, build a house, get some pigs and cows and be neighbourly with folks. I don't want to be fighting all the time. Be hating and hated all the time."

"Your paw'd shoot you if he heard this," she said.

"That's how it is with me, anyway. I don't like going to Osage. Folks stare and I know what they're thinking. Ellie, *I* don't hate *them.*"

"A stone house near a creek, Carl?"

"About likc that, I rcckon. With a root cellar and a place to put down salted meat and apples, eggs, in a salt-crock."

"And a woman?"

He nodded, blood coming into his face.

"To lie with?"

He got up swiftly and stared at her. "Ellie; you ought to be ashamed."

"You can't use a boar if you're going to have young," she said harshly and jumped up with her back to him. "They go with the house and all."

"You shouldn't talk like that though."

"Why not? Matthew and Judith Anne do. They do worse than talk about it, because I *know*."

"Well," he said and gulped and looked down her back where the curve and swell of strong flesh was. "Well, I just felt like I wanted to tell you how it was with me, is all."

"Carl?"

"Yes."

"When are you going to do it—go away?"

"I don't know. It's what I *want* to do. I haven't made no plans exactly. Not yet."

She faced around. He was surprised at the strange, urgent expression she wore. There was something cunning and secretive in her face he'd never seen there before. Like she was smoothing out an idea, perfecting it as she stared at him. Like a man might look bent over a beaver trap, baiting it, working it all out in his mind beforehand.

"I guess what Matthew and Judith Anne do isn't wrong. I guess she knows what she's doing," Ellie said.

"You're talking strange, Ellie. I never heard you talk like this before."

"Maybe you haven't," she said. "I reckon I had to grow up sometime. Learn to see things different. Like they really are in life. Not bad or good, but like they really are."

"Well, anyway," he said, retreating before

her strangeness, "I feel better after telling you how it is with me. I guess that's because you didn't call me down about it." He was trying to get things back like they had been, but in this he was outmatched. The black fire in her stare blinded him. His words trailed off into stillness.

She went very close to him, until the rise and fall of her blouse brushed against his shirt-front and there was a challenge in her face as clear as the sky; as inviting as a cool pool. "I want to go away too," she said. "Maybe even out of the Territory. I hadn't thought where, but away."

"You do?"

"Just away. And have things of my own. A stone house by a creek. I've pictured it in my mind, Carl. With critters around, and young ones."

She took his hand and pressed it deep in the valley of her breasts and leaned up against him like that, with the tall, thin shadows mottling them and the curse of unhappiness almost a physical pain in them both.

Carl made no move to draw away; he was rooted. A spiral of warmth uncoiled in him, thrust upwards and upwards and he finally forgot what, exactly, he wanted from life and thought only of the agonising want that was there in the shady glade with them, beside the

39

muddling creek, and touched her hair with his free hand. Let it wind through the blackness, fingers like brown worms, groping without sight. Then dropped his hand lower, to her neck, to her shoulder, and let it hand there.

She was as still as stone, but the hard thrust when she breathed, burst against him so he knew there was more than his own wanton fever between them. Kept his hand upon her shoulder, afraid; almost sick with fear, with knees that trembled, with sweat that ran and nearly blinded him.

She was biting her lip and it hurt, but not enough to make her cry, but she cried anyway, softly. Racking-deep, but softly, and when he moved back a little she sank down limply on the grass-hummock and covered her face with her hands and just cried.

"Ellie . . . ?"

He was miserable, the fire burnt to ashes; dropped down beside her and when she looked at him through her fingers, he was long-faced, as white as a sheet with his mouth hanging slack, dark lashes half covering his eyes.

"Carl; are you ashamed?"

"Yes."

"I'm not." She wiped her face. It felt hot. She pressed palms against her cheeks and when he glanced up her eyes were twice as black as he'd ever seen them. There was an unearthly lustre to them from the tears.

"You cried," he said.

"I don't know why. Maybe I was too upset. Maybe because when you want something a lot, and it comes close, you can't stand it."

"Want what?"

"That house by the creek and the man who'll make it for me."

He stared at her.

"That's why I cried. Carl? Will you kiss me. I want you to kiss me."

When he didn't move she slid off the hummock and got close to him, reached up with both hands and kissed him on the mouth, on the lips, pulled back six inches and looked at him and smiled, then she kissed him again and Carl couldn't remember ever having seen Ellie Parkinson smile before, although he *had* seen her smile because they'd grown up together. There had been lots of things they'd snickered over. Only—this was a smile; a *real* smile. It meant more than humour; in fact there really wasn't any humour to it. It meant something much greater than humour and he knew he'd never seen her *smile* before.

"I've got some meat in my saddlebags," she said, her face no more than a foot from his. "Shall I get it?"

41

"I couldn't eat," he said candidly.

"This is food," she said, and pressed her wide lips over his mouth, held him in a velvet grip so that he couldn't have torn free if his life had depended upon it. Then she lay her head against him and the furry quiver of her breath touched his neck and he groped with his hands, locked them around her.

"I know how a bird feels when you hold it in your hand." she said softly. "Now I know exactly how it feels." She took one of his hands. "Do you feel my heart?"

"Yes."

She put his hand down again and pressed her own fingers against his chest. "And yours . . ."

"I don't feel right, Ellie."

"Scairt?"

"More'n just scairt. Like this is wrong."

She made a hard, short shake of her head and the lash of her hair made his skin prickle. "No it isn't. I thought so too, for a while, but I know now it's not wrong. We're both straining to get the things we want. That's not wrong."

"Well, no," he said, "*that* ain't—but *this* might be."

"No, not even this, because it's you and me. Your paw, my paw . . . Matthew and Judith Anne . . . The people at the settlement . . .

None of them matter right now. There's nothing but you and me and what we do with each other is right. That's what I was thinking a while back when I turned my back on you. What you and I do together is right." She plucked at the back of his shirt where it hung soggily against him. "You're sweating like a stud-horse."

"I got reason."

She stiffened the length of her, drew back, got to her feet and reached down to tug him off the ground. "Come along. Come down a ways."

The creek slapped torpidly against some grey sand. Sunshine exploded off tiny pebbles and the ground underfoot was soggy, spongy.

"Lie down there. No; take your shirt off first."

"What for?" But he removed it and the breadth of his chest was immense, swelling upwards and outwards from lean flanks, corded and thick from labour. But paler than his wrists and face where the sun had left its shades.

"Now lie down there; on your stomach."

And she scooped up water in her hands and washed his back with slow, circling motions. Bent over him and leaned with her upper body swaying until his head, lying over his arms, grew limp and began to sway, too.

It was wonderful. It was cooling and relaxing. It was a blissfulness he succumbed readily to. Neither of them spoke for a long time. Until the shadows had moved a little, south-and-west, then she kissed him between the shoulder blades, up along the neck and he rolled over to reach for her with all the fright gone. Touched her with the tremors stilled, the doubts and quaking forgotten, and she smiled tenderly at him.

"Matthew told Judith Anne you're all going to Osage tomorrow. I'm coming to you there, Carl, and we're going away."

He heard through a redness and didn't care what she said; what anyone said. Nothing remained for him but the bigness of her eyes, growing bigger, until she closed them.

When he got back the shadows were long and his mother said she had some venison gruel, but the thought gagged him and he went out to the well, drank a dipper full of cold water instead. Watched the azure sky darken with brassy tints out along its frayed edges; was still standing there when Matthew reined a skittery colt across the yard all flecked with sudsy foam and darkened with nervousness, like colts get when they're new to man and the saddle.

Watched Matthew dismount, grunt something to the grunt shadow working over a wagon just inside the barn's doorway, then turn and gaze towards the well where Carl was standing.

Matthew unsaddled by feel, pulled off the rigging and heaved it over a corral stringer. Turned the colt loose inside and crossed the yard with spurs ringing. Carl drew a dipper full of water and held it out. Their eyes locked over it, Matthew's piercing-clear and knowing in an ironic way, Carl's murky in their depths, like windswept ashes.

"Find her?" Matthew asked over the dipper.

"Yes. She was all right."

"I reckon she was," Matthew said and smiled his secret smile.

"Give me a hand with these wheels," the Old Man called from the barn. They went over and lifted. There was yellowish tallow on the spindles, new washers of thick leather. They set the wagon down when the Old Man had the wheels back on. The Old Man knelt to twist up the burrs.

"Going to the settlement?" Matthew asked, as though he didn't know; as though nothing core-like lay between him and the Old Man.

"Sunup," the Old Man said, twisting until

cords leapt out in the backs of his hands, in the wrists. "I'll take your maw over to Parkinson's shortly."

The boys nodded, for it had always been like that; their mother would not go to Osage. When it was necessary to go, the Old Man left her with the Parkinsons until they got back, and just the three men went.

The thought of his father at Parkinson's made Carl's throat go dry. He went back over by the well. Matthew crossed to his side idly, remembering the Old Man's austerity and coldness and considering it in silence.

Carl said: "We can do the chores while he's gone."

"Yeh."

By the time the Old Man got back it was full night. There was a thin gash of moon and little undernourished stars. The sky itself was tuck-belly blue, sort of purplish. The heat had gone with the sun and it was balmy with a high-running wind blowing like a sigh, overhead. It was unusual for winds to blow in midsummer. As the three big men moved in the rickety lamplight in the house, none heeded or heard that wind. Each was withdrawn from the other. Not one face, but that sought shadows, away from the orange glow, secretive, apart.

Carl was last to bed. For hours he lay on his

back looking upwards. Blind with his eyes wide open. He was very still and except for the strange wind, so was the stone house.

Ellie—Ellie . . . I got drowning shame in me, Ellie, but I'm proud. Life flowed from me. Life to grow warm and moving. It sort of overpowers my mind, Ellie . . .

The day came, strangely hazy with an ashen sky and a high mist that scudded before the sun like gauze. A very strange day and the Old Man stood in the yard looking at it with sweat bursting out under his clothing, because, in spite of the haziness, it was stifling-hot. He would remember this day and not only for its unusualness.

"Ready?"

"Ready," Matthew said picking up the lines, flicking them.

"Rifles in, Carl?"

"Yes."

"Plenty of everything?" That meant for trouble and they all knew it, even if the Old Man didn't say so.

"Plenty of everything," Matthew said and they rolled out of the yard with the Old Man still peering around at the odd weather moving his lips every once in a while without making a sound.

He looked like a scarecrow, all weather-checked and scruffy, until you saw his face,

47

then you completely lost the vision of an old scarecrow and never again did he look like one to you, in spite of his gauntness, his big-framed gauntness. There was something in his face.

The wagon creaked, jolted along. They avoided scrub-oak clumps, staying well in the open. They were without cover and the heat was thick, oppressive, and the team raised yellow dust, which choked them. They got thirsty and there was no water. No one spoke. It was in their weal to suffer, to accept discomfort without comment. Morning waned, the land bumped past, heat shimmered and except for the creaking, groaning of the wagon, there was no sound.

Driving now at a jangling trot, now at a plodding walk, Matthew sank low into memory. The vividness of his secret was never far and usually he re-lived it with relish. Today he did not. Other times he'd crawled into it and moulted there, all limp and relaxed. Today, its refuge was painful, for in the background of that shadowed luridness was a great gaunt phantom, staring. Watching and staring.

He spat clotted dust and tooled the wagon without effort, hunched over, probing eyes slitted and never still.

Carl sprawled on the splintery wagonbed behind the seat where his father and brother rode and looked vacantly at the parched land, the gauzy sky, the brittleness of a worn and dusty world. Thought of Ellie and quickening life and how things grew.

Finally, with shirts sweat-darkened, faces flushed from heat, they arrived on the out-skirts of the settlement. It was tame country to them. Where men wielded hoes and hammers and lived all bunched together like a tribe. There were things to see, like women with fantastically bustled hips and waists so tiny any Fenwick would crush them with one hand. And men with long hair and greasy pants of antelope-skin. And glass in some of the windows.

"Tie up near the trough," the Old Man said.

Matthew guidcd thc tcam to the ragged old cottonwood, scarred man-high with teeth marks from hundreds of cribbing horses. Next to the scraggly trunk, the water-trough was big and iron-bound and full of ill water, green around the edges. An iron pump pointed its snout down to the water at the far end and flies in the trillions ran uphill and downhill all day where the horses had stood swishing tails in the tree's shade.

The Old Man worked the pump in stony silence. Matthew and Carl drank, let water spill over their faces, down under their shirts,

49

then the Old Man did likewise and they all stood erect, big mastiffs, sniffing, feeling the place. Letting its noise and smell sift through their pores.

The Old Man hitched at his shell-belt and chipped old pistol, rubbed wet palms along the edges of his pants and said, "I'm going to the emporium. Meet me there when you're through lookin' around—and remember—stay together."

He started across the road with dust squirting from beneath his boots. Carl leaned on the wagon and Matthew looked at people. Several men slowed along the plankwalk, gazed back, and one stopped in mid-stride to stare at them; the big men, the warped old wagon, the whipcord-hard team, under the tree. Three rifles slanted upwards against the back of the wagon's seat.

"There's Harry Cumberland," Matthew said, and Carl turned to look.

"What's he staring at?"

"Us," Matthew said, watching the preacher turn slowly and move off. "I guess he's surprised to see us in the settlement."

Carl watched Cumberland walk away without speaking. He didn't dislike Preacher Harry, and he didn't like him. It was enough for Carl that such men were alive, like cactus spines. You didn't spend yourself hating such men, fighting them; you just didn't bother yourself over them. You just watched, said little, and avoided them.

Carl was still watching Cumberland when the preacher paused across and down the road a ways where a lethargic crowd of men stood. Some were whittling with their hats tilted forward, some were talking and gesturing, none very animated. Harry spoke to several of the loiterers, but what piqued Carl was the crowd itself.

"What's going on down there?"

Matthew looked, and knew the mud building behind the crowd. "They got someone in jail, most likely. 'Look like a posse that's just come back all tuckered out."

Carl considered this and found it plausible. "I wonder who they got? Maybe that Ponca Indian folks been talking about."

"Maybe. Let's go see."

Matthew began to move out from the tree-shade. Carl followed slowly and neither of them paid any attention to the fact that Preacher Harry was still down there, talking to men in the crowd.

They crossed the road, stepped up onto the plankwalk and started southward, dwarfing those they passed. At the jailhouse, men looked up at them, neither nodded or spoke and Harry Cumberland planted his legs wide

51

with his back to them, silent, unmoving, re-
mindful of a porpupine, bristles-up-waiting.

"Who's in there?" Matthew asked a wiz-
ened Texan with a big silver star on his hip-
holster and an agelessness to his crinkled
brown face that came from desert living and
constant dehydration.

"Kid Marcy." The Texan squinted upwards.

"That so? Who's he?" Carl asked.

The Texan's hand-knife hovered over the
peg he was whittling. "Quantrill man—
among other things. Killer an' rustler an'
stage robber."

Matthew moved closer to a high, slotted
window, deeply recessed in the massive mud
wall. He and his brother were the only men in
the crowd tall enough to peer in without
raising up. Carl pressed close.

The man sitting on a straw-pallet in a shadowed corner of the cell was slight of build,
lean to the point of emaciation. His eyes
glowed with a steady, pale light.

"Not over nineteen," Carl said.

Kid Marcy's head moved. He looked at
them through the steel straps woven over the
little window. Stared without interest or hope
or even venom; just stared. "Twenty-four," he
said.

"You got yourself in a mess," Matthew said

to him. "Too bad."

Marcy made a dry grin at Matthew. "Ain't it too bad, though? But it ain't important, stranger. It ain't important at all. Not when you get right down to the meat of it."

"What'll they do to you?"

"Why, hang me, of course," Marcy said. "What else can they do?"

"That's important," Matthew said solemnly. "It sure as hell would be to me—if I was in there."

"What would you do about it?" Marcy asked, lounging back along the wall with his quirked-up little grin; sleepy looking, heavy lidded with his mouth open like he was listening to something no one else could hear.

"First off they wouldn't have me in there," Matthew said. "Second off—I'd sure tussle before I'd let them hang me."

"Aw, it ain't that important," Marcy said again. "Nothing folks do is important. Folks are here, on earth, stuck like. What they do's like what ants do. How many thousands of folks you seen—and what's left of them? What they done and thought? They're handiest of animals, maybe, but they can't go no farther than their age, can they? Even the littlest pebble in the creek's more lasting. Amounts to more. A feller dies a little bit each day moving closer to the biggest thing in his

53

life. Death. *That's* important, the *man* ain't. Did you see the war, stranger?"

Carl was pressing his face close. "No," he said.

"Well, I did. I see how folks die, how everything they make crumbles away; rots; so I know it ain't important."

"Ain't you afraid of being hung?"

"Naw; why should I be? I'm going to die — that's the only thing I'll ever do that matters. It's the biggest thing I *can* do."

"Don't you have any friends?" Carl asked, stirred deeper than he knew by something he'd never dreamt existed; a philosophy of fatalism, of defeat, of nihilism.

"Sure, I got friends. A man's got to have friends. Four eyes are better'n two. I got friends, but now I split off from them. They ain't come to *theirs* yet, and I have. That's all there is to that."

"What did you do?" Matthew asked.

"I killed a man for his money."

"In cold blood?"

Marcy shrugged. "I reckon. He was reaching for his rifle under the buggyseat."

"How'd you get caught?"

"Fellers working cattle over the hill from the road heard me shoot."

A moment of silence ensued while the young men stared at one another. Of the three,

54

Kid Marcy was the least moved. There was noise around him. The buzzing of tail-winding flies sleek and fat, of men's voices in a summer-drawl.

Someone reached up and brushed fingers across Carl's shoulder and he turned, looked down. Behind the bearded man who had touched him stood Harry Cumberland and a little knot of watchers, all grim-faced like brownstone. The air was charged with something thick and stale-like.

"Are you the Fenwick brothers?" the bearded man asked.

"Yes; I'm Carl. This is my brother, Matthew."

"I'm Bunsen. Pete Bunsen, the sheriff. I want a word with the two of you."

Matthew was peering into the sheriff's face. "All right," he said, "talk."

"At my place," Bunsen said. "Come along."

They walked with Bunsen, dwarfing him in everything but breadth and coldness, for the sheriff had a face like iron and two small eyes brighter than turquoise. His jaw was square, his head bullet-shaped under an old rusty hat. There was an aura of deadliness about him; you could almost smell it in his sweat.

"In here. Sit down over there. Now then; what do the both of you know about Will Parson?"

Matthew, got up off the bench he'd just dropped down upon. The look he gave Bunsen was ice over ferment.

"Nothing," he said. "Harry Cumberland came to see us a couple of months back, saying someone here in the settlement said we'd stolen Parson's four-years-olds. That's a lie."

"Is it?" Bunsen asked, standing across a dirty table from them. "There's folks say you killed Parson, too. Is that another lie, Fenwick?"

"Kill him? We didn't even know he was dead."

Bunsen's bearded face took on a harshness that glowed like fire. Fervour gouged the lines deeper when he squinted at them. "I get tired listenin' to lies and liars," he said. "Sick and tired of it." He looked down at Carl, who was still seated, saw the astonished expression there, the large, dark-ringed eyes with their moving depths, and returned his attention to Matthew who was the kind of man Peter Bunsen understood; big and rough and armed, as hard in the face as Fight, as powerful as Might. A knot bulged in Bunsen's throat while blood sang in his head, for Matthew was temptation, like whisky was madness, and to a killing man, both were a challenge.

"The law needs just one thing to try a man—witnesses to his crime. I got 'em."

"That we killed Parson? Why, my God," Matthew said, "we hardly knew him."

"But he talked against you, didn't he? You heard he was talkin' against you."

"We never heard any such a damned thing. My brother and me scarcely knew Will Parson when we seen him. The Old Man knew him a little, but—"

"The Old Man's the string behind the bow, ain't he?"

"What do you mean?"

"He's the one leads you, ain't he? Now tell me he's never took you out after cattle that belonged to other folks. Now tell me that damned lie, too."

"There's nothing wrong in taking Yankee cattle; during the war they took ours."

"The war's over."

"Go find me a Texan that believes that."

"This ain't Texas and I ain't here to argue. When you come to Osage today, you figured folks'd be scairt and hightail it—but they didn't, did they? This has been three months building up and you Fenwicks thought it was all over. Thought folks'd forgot, or were too scairt of you to do anything."

At last Carl got up off the bench. He looked at the closed door, listening.

"Bunsen's eyes saw this without leaving Matthew's face for the sheriff knew which of them was most deadly. "Those voices you're listening to," he said,. "belong to the folks you thought'd run as soon as you come to town. Well; they ain't running. They're the hang-rope party. If you doubt me, just open that damned door and look out. That's the people and the people are the law—don't you forget it. Now turn around and lean against the wall an' put your hands up it as far as you can reach!"

CHAPTER THREE

The Old Man was taken without a struggle. Ringed around with guns and curses and rough abuse that left marks on his jaw and deeper, in his soul, where fury was more than half.

He met Matthew and Carl with cries against the three of them, drowning out what Carl said through twisted lips and importuning eyes, and with Osage in a sweaty furore over their "capture."

The booming preachments of Harry Cumberland, beard flying with the rabid workings of his jaw and spittle flecking it silver while he roared for doom, was loud above all else. Down in the crowd, back where the dust hung, stood a little woman named Widow Harris. She looked at Preacher Harry with awe and emotion and a dampness that made the dust stick to her little face. His thundering quivered in her head.

And in the corner of the mud-walled cell, Kid Marcy sat, looking at them with keen pale eyes and a crooked little grin. When the Old Man saw him there, thin and wispy like a straw doll cast aside, he ignored him. There was a black look of murder in the Old Man's face and nothing mattered to him but fury. Carl brushed a hand over the Old Man's sleeve and it was shaken off.

Matthew stepped in front of him. "Did Bunsen tell you why he did this? About Will Parson?"

"He told me," the Old Man said fiercely, "but it ain't that. It's a world of things. Harry Cumberland's the biggest part. Him and gossip." The Old Man balled his fist and glared at Matthew. "Now you know why I never took to settlements. It's the people . . . like wolves."

"They got this law—"

"Law of tooth and fang! Now shut up, I got to think."

Unheeding, Carl spoke up. "What do they figure to do with us?"

Kid Marcy's laugh, reedy, came into the

dwindling bedlam from outside. "Hang you. Take you to the cottonwood tree by the water trough and strangle you till your tongue's out a foot."

The Old Man whirled. "Who are you?" When Marcy told him he flung down a scorning curse and turned away. "Scum; Secesh scum,' he said.

Marcy's grin faded. "You weren't Secesh?" he asked.

"I wasn't neither. I never owned a nigger—why should I fight to keep 'em or give 'em away? I was for myself and mine; minded my own business."

"You got beliefs, oldtimer?"

"What I got," the Old Man stormed, "is no business of yours. Keep quiet."

The Kid kept quiet. He was unarmed and small. They were three and swollen with power. But he listened.

The day lost itself. Sunlight shown against the east side of the mud-wattle jailhouse and the air became more foetid than ever as dusk settled and osage grew tired, went home to eat and nod.

Carl stood by the little window, peered out through the steel slats. The land far out had the sun's colour caught, was spreading it thinly so that there was a broad belt of lambent flame stretching from the last hovel on the outskirts to the farthest hills, dimly visible through haze. The world was blurred in endless refraction and the strain, the tumult, was gone from the day. There was peacefulness far out, he could sense it.

"Paw; we got to get out of here."

The Old Man looked up from where he sat on the dirt floor and regarded Carl's back caustically. "With wings?"

"No, with guns and help."

The Old Man's posture was leashed stillness. There was a twisting, a wrenching, inside him which was only visible in his sunken eyes. He made a short grunt of scorn and looked down again and over by the window Carl sensed the contempt. Recognised it, because he'd felt it hundreds of times before. Only this time it mattered; not because it hurt, but because when he spoke again the Old Man would stare at him. Because the Old Man had sight—would sense the truth as soon as Carl spoke.

But there was no struggle, really, for Carl wanted life. Wanted a chance to touch it, mould it as it grew, thrill to its mystery, so he turned with his back to the window and sunlight glowed around his head.

"Ellie was coming to me in the settlement today," he said. "She'll be out there some place right now, and when she hears what happened she'll come here."

The Old Man's head lifted like Carl had known it would, but the silence lasted longer than he'd thought. The Old Man glared at him, and Carl looked to see his brother staring rigidly at the wall and hugging his knees close. Then he turned back and the Old Man's stare was distantly frozen.

"You too?"

Carl failed to understand.

"You and Ellie?"

Matthew squirmed, hugged his legs tighter and slowly came around to face their father. There was ice in his eyes. "Leave him be," he said.

"Shut up! I know about you. I seen that."

"Yeh, you seen it! You told us to take what's been denied us, but when we take it—"

"*Shut up!*"

Over in his corner, Kid Marcy's eyes glowed with strange, hot interest. He was thinly motionless.

The Old Man's chest rose and fell while he stared at his youngest, who ventured words into the silence.

"All right, you know. I ain't ashamed. I *wanted* it to be that way and I ain't ashamed of it, but right now I'm not thinkin' about that; I'm thinking about getting out of here. Ellie'll find us. She'll help."

The Old Man listened without looking at any of them. When Matthew spoke, with the fierceness gone from his voice, the Old Man shook himself gently, like a dog coming out of Chagrin Creek and spread his hands palms downward in the dust and paid attention.

"She'd better hurry," he said hollowly. "I know settlement people. Soon's their guts are full in the morning they'll drag us out of here."

Kid Marcy laughed. It startled the others. The Old Man's brows drew down thunderously. "What's funny?" he demanded.

"You," the Kid said.

Matthew came up off the ground with a growl, his bigness multiplied in the dying light, and Kid Marcy looked at him oddly, understanding instantly what even Matthew had never completely understood. That while Matthew was strong in the mind by himself, and would do things his own way, in his own time, with grim stubbornness, he would also yield to the Old Man, and it wasn't pitiable, it was uncommon and great that he did this, for he was mighty and reckless and full of lust and bravery, so it wasn't servility or fear. It was devotion so deep he didn't even know it himself, and that was a sacred thing. The Kid watched him come across the room and

63

grinned up at him with no defence and no fear either.

"Remember what I said about it not bein' important what we do or think or when we die?"

Matthew stopped and the Old Man looked over and Carl shuffled his feet, while something strange and quickening possessed his mind.

"Well; that's what's funny to me. The Old Man's there's so mad about something else he's close to destroying all three of you over it. If the girl comes it won't surprise me if he spits in her face and makes her go away—and you'll all get hung because he feels that way. Ain't that funny, big feller?"

Matthew stood glaring a moment longer then he went back to his corner, a shaggy lion in a too-small cage. For a time there was utter silence, then the Old Man spoke.

"We'll survive," he said to his sons, and there was godhood in their father to them both. They regarded him with belief, never doubting, so when Ellie came and leaned against the warm mud wall in the blackest of the night, they talked to her and she passed them two derringers she'd carried in her clothing and they told her to steal four saddled horses from somewhere and tie them out in the dark, and then to wait.

Kid Marcy spoke from his corner, a voice and a blur of pinched face. "Make it five horses, boys.," he said, "and I'll get you enough Yankee dollars to patch hell a mile."

Matthew glanced stonily at his father. Carl had eyes only for Ellie's still and frightened face below the sill.

The Old Man said, "Five horses, girl, and when you get them, make a night-bird call from across the way."

Ellie faded into the stillness. Carl strained to see her. Matthew and the Old Man went over to Kid Marcy and hunkered close. It was so dark, none of them could see more than the barest outlines. The Old Man could not be still. He squirmed and fondled the big-bored little gun and kept twisting his head to peer in the direction of the cell door.

Kid Marcy spoke in a brisk voice, unlike the tone he'd used before. "Getting out's the main thing," he said. "If we get separated it don't matter much. Keep moving, don't stop and rest or nothing. They'll be hunting us like wolves so keep moving. If you miss the horses don't spend time looking for them, grab another, double back, keep moving, keep running. We got the night and that's about all we have got. That and motion. I know what I'm talking about; I been through this ten dozen times—*you got to keep moving*. That's the secret of escape." He paused and looked at them.

"Now then; there's a guard sleeps on a cot outside the door. I'll be sick if you fellers call him in here. Don't shoot him, it'll make too much noise." He stopped again. "Give me one of the pistols."

"No!" The Old Man hissed, burning gaze rife with suspicion.

The Kid was checked up a moment, then he shrugged. "All right; I'll get a gun. Now when we get to the horses, you fellers got to follow me. I know where we can hide." He stopped speaking suddenly and looked at them. "You don't mean to take that girl, along, do you?"

Carl loomed up. "We do. We do or don't none of us leave this cell."

The Old Man craned his neck, like he hadn't heard right. Matthew ignored it, reached out and touched the Kid's knee. "Follow you where? We know this country better'n anyone does. We got a ranch ten miles out, and a stone house."

Marcy considered this a moment, then he said, "I got friends in the Cherokee Nation." It was enough, for every man knew the 'Nation was a realm of renegades and outlaws; that no lawman dared ride there. Even the Army rarely made excursions into those hills and empty fastnesses for what spies didn't warn against ahead of time, crafty hidden ambushers killed later.

The Old Man leaned forward and spoke with hushed vehemence. "No! We'll ride for our own place. If you want to come along you're welcome, but we ain't outlaws."

Marcy drew off the wall. "You damned old fool, they'll hit your place the first thing."

"Let 'em! It's been hit before and no man ever took a one of us from it."

Marcy looked into the fanatical eyes a moment, then turned to gaze at Matthew, on to Carl. There was bold confidence in each face. For a while then, he thought. The 'Nation was a long three days ride to boot. For a while then; until I rest up. Aloud, he said, "All right; we'll head for your place."

A night-bird trilled, a lost and lonely sound.

Marcy craned his thin neck. "Is that girl an Indian?" He asked, and when no one answered him he got up, listened by the door a moment, then crumpled all soddenly in the centre of the room groaning and threshing so realistically the Old Man marvelled and Matthew's sombre eyes glinted. Carl moved farther back by the window, shot a glance outward, moved his lips without speaking then looked down at the wretch on the floor again.

"Whadda hell's goin' on in there? You fellers been to fightin'?"

The door swung back a crack. Lamplight sprang inside, a thin line of hope. The opening widened and the jailer stood there sleep-swollen and dishevelled, looking down at the Kid.

"What happened to him? Some one of you knife 'im?"

"He's sick," the Old Man said very deliberately, watching the scattergun and lamp in the jailer's hands. "Ever since we come in here he's been moaning and groaning. Looks to me like he's been poisoned—all clutching up like that."

The light showed streaked sweat and dust on the Kid's face. His eyes were rolled back and saliva like yellow rust trickled from his mouth. When Carl looked more closely he was struck and awed by the realism, of it, not totally believing it *was* acting.

"Get him some water," the Old Man said. "Ain't there a doctor you can get?"

The jailer looked at the three of them and said, "Move back. Over by the back wall. I got to drag him outside. Get back, damn you. Move!"

He shuffled closer to the Kid and held the lantern out, peering, then he put the light down and stopped with his free hand ex-

68

extended, fingers made crooked to grasp the Kid's belt and the Old Man said: "Don't move!"

The jailer rolled his eyes upwards, saw the wicked little guns and became a bent statue, fingers still hooked, arm extended. Once, his tongue darted out and in, that was all.

"Give the Kid his pistol," the Old Man said to Matthew who moved forward. "Carl; take his riot-gun. Carl, you—"

"He's mine," the Kid said, sitting up and reaching for the jailer's hip-holster. He got the gun and arose all in one smooth motion, arm swinging. The jailer broke the lantern when he fell across it.

"Come on!"

The roadside door was barred from the inside. When the Kid opened it there was blackness outside as thick and cloying as the darkness inside. He slipped through and the Fenwicks followed.

The night-bird sounded again.

Carl made straight for it across the roadway without heeding anything else. The Old Man hissed something, but Matthew was following after so he nudged the Kid and they all crossed to where Ellie met them. She had a rifle in her hand and held it out to Carl when he stepped up onto the plankwalk.

"Here, Carl."

"Where're the horses, lady?" the Kid asked swiftly.

She led them down a tight passage between rickety buildings and into a littered alleyway, then looked anxiously back before she turned south. The horses were tied beneath a smooth Bois d'Arc. She was still carrying the rifle and when Carl handed her some reins, she had to shift the weapon to take them.

"Where, Carl?"

"Home."

"Who's that other man?"

"His name's Kid Marcy. He killed a man."

"Oh; that's him. I heard folks talking about him."

They rode hard behind the Old Man. He just naturally led them, as leary as an old cougar and as silent. He kept swinging his head from side to side and once in a while he'd rein up to listen.

There was no sound of pursuit, but his vigil never slackened. The burning gaze didn't soften until dawn came, a long bloody streak across the gut of heaven. By then they were miles out. The Old Man drew up, put his hands across the saddlehorn and sat there.

"Kid," he said, watching back where emptiness lay. "Are you a believing man?"

"A what?"

The sunken eyes swung closer, to Marcy's

70

face, thin and small and whisker-shadowed. "You wouldn't be," the Old Man said. "It don't matter anyhow. We're here—we survived. That's what matters. Now you can ride to the 'Nation and your friends, or if you've a mind, you can trail along with us. Either way there'll be trouble for you, I warrant you that."

"I'll trail along."

The Old Man looked at Ellie before he lifted the reins. "It don't matter," he said. "There's plenty of evil with us already. A little more won't matter."

He pushed on and they followed him. Kid Marcy fell back beside Carl, who was riding with Ellie. He meant to speak, but Carl's face dissuaded him. The three of them rode glumly behind Matthew, steeped in silence.

When they swung past the stone house the Old Man drew up, watched the others climb down. "Girl," he said, "don't get off. Ride on home. When you get there tell my wife to get back here as fast as she can. Tell your paw what's happened—and I hope he flays you alive. Now go on."

Carl flung around the side of the horse he'd been riding, face working and deathly pale, so that his eyes seemed half out of his head.

"Leave her be!"

"*Shut up!*"

Matthew saw the saliva bubble on his

71

father's mouth. He grabbed Carl and whirled him around. Without speaking, they were inches apart. Kid Marcy was motionless, watching, no expression on his face. There was that which was so different between the sons, but it was Matthew who could sway Carl. He did it now, without lifting a hand or speaking a word.

"Get—girl!"

Ellie's face was flushed and haggard, but spirit shone in the black eyes. Kid Marcy saw her fully for the first time. He didn't take his eyes off her until she'd ridden out of sight around the house.

"Cut the reins off at the bit," the Old Man said, "and chouse them out of the yard." He meant the stolen horses, but he wasn't looking at them. He finally turned his own animal and drove the loose stock away in a wild run, stirrups flopping. Marcy and the Fenwick boys watched him until he slid to a halt, got down, cut his own reins and threw clods at the horses until they fled. Then the Old Man came trudging back.

Matthew stopped at the well for a drink. Carl went past to the house and Kid Marcy waited for the Old Man. When he got close the Kid said, "This ain't very far out—what makes you think they won't come after us here?"

"They'll come. They'll be riding after us right now, but it won't do them any good." He turned, cocked his head, then scowled and muttered something.

The Kid looked from the Old Man to the stone house. "They'll tie us down in there, oldtimer. The way to escape is to keep moving. I know."

"Do you?" The Old Man said, glaring fully at Marcy. "Well; me and mine don't run. We ain't committed no crime and we don't run."

The Kid seemed unimpressed by the Old Man's wrath. "You didn't learn back there, did you? *You can't argue with a rope.*"

"If you're scairt keep on going."

"Scairt? I'm not scairt." The Kid laughed in his reedy way and looked over where Matthew was slumped against the well-box. "I don't give a damn one way or the other— why should I be scairt?"

"You talk like you are."

"Look, old man," the Kid said. His gun came out and up in a blur. There was a crashing explosion, a burst of feathers where a low-flying bird had been. "That's how scairt I am; see how my hand was shaking?"

The Old Man was unimpressed. "That proves nothing," he said. "I judge a man after two days without water—after ten days inside a forted up house with red devils screaching

73

around outside." He nodded towards the holstered gun. "Either of my boys can do that."

Marcy looked after the Old Man who strode across the yard. There was wonderment in his gaze.

"Is the water barrel full, Carl?"

"It's full."

"Everything else ready?"

"Everything's ready."

Matthew came through the doorway, had to drop his head to do so. He looked at his brother for a space before he came on into the gloomy big room. Carl was sitting on a bench cradling his rifle. His face was ashen, mouth slack and damp. Matthew crossed over to him and Kid Marcy, standing watch near the door with his lopsided grin fixed in place, peered outward where the deafening cymbal-crash of blazing hot stillness lay.

"Carl; she couldn't have stayed. He was right in sending her after maw."

"He's crazy, Matthew. We're going to fight them. This is crazy. It was different before— when Harry Cumberland came. That time we hadn't broke any of their laws; this time we have."

"But hell, Carl, we had to. Didn't any of us kill Will Parson, you know that. We ain't done any wrong. They'd have hung us if we hadn't busted out of there."

"They think we killed Parson. You remember what their sheriff said. The people are the law. You know what the people think of us. Why did we stop here? Why didn't we just keep on going?" Carl looked over where the Old Man was loading guns and muttering to himself. "He *wants* to fight 'em, Matthew. He's going to bottle us all up in here and make a hell of a fight out of this."

"If we run they'll never let us stop running, Carl."

"If we was to run far enough . . ."

The sun climbed steadily higher. It was so big and pale yellow, the whole sky seemed filled with it and you couldn't look up or when you looked back down there was blindness and speckles in front of your eyes. But it was cool inside, gloomily so. The two-foot thick stone walls made it like that. A mud-soddy roof aided.

Over by the flung-back door the Kid said, "Riders coming from the southeast. Can't see them yet, but it don't sound like very many."

The Old Man raised his head, tilted it, then crossed to the doorway. "The Parkinsons," he said, squinting outward. Then he said, "Where's my wife?"

"One of them's that same girl, oldtimer."

The Old Man turned swiftly. "My name's Jacob Fenwick—you remember that."

75

The Kid's glance left Ellie only long enough to flicker over the gaunt bigness close to him. He said nothing.

"Matthew; fetch them inside. Have John put the horses in the barn." As Matthew squeezed past, his father said in a low tone, "If you so much as touch her, I'll lock you out!"

Matthew went on by like he hadn't heard and Kid Marcy looked after him in a puzzled way.

Jacob went back to the gloom and turned his back, fell to working over the assortment of guns he had laid out. There was a terrible foreboding in him, so that his hands shook, but none could see that.

When the others were nearing the door he turned, watched them file into the room. John Parkinson and his sinful girls; that was all.

Dark and massive, Parkinson crossed to the Old Man's side, gazed down at the laid-out guns and up into the Old Man's face. He touched a musket with his fingers.

"She's left you, Jacob. Went yesterday."

The Old Man's voice was low and clear. "Where?"

"To her kinfolk in Missouri."

"Why?"

"She said there was only one she'd loved—

the one that died. She come over here, got a bundle of his stuff and rode off. I couldn't make her stop."

Parkinson continued to stroke the black-oily rifle with one hand and the Old Man stood like a ramrod over their heads, and while Kid Marcy kept his vigil at the doorway, unknowing, both Carl and Matthew listened heads-down to what the Parkinson girls had to tell them. They said nothing and the Old Man turned his back upon them all and bent over the guns. John Parkinson's gaze hung to his face.

"I did what I could, Jacob."

"I'll hear no more about it," the Old Man said.

Parkinson looked down at the guns. "You aim to stand them off?"

"Yes. Alone if need be."

Parkinson looked around the room, felt the fateful silence. "You can't do it, Jacob."

"Why can't I? Give me one reason."

"Well, God A'mighty, these ain't Indians," the 'breed said explosively. "They'll set up a siege an' starve you out."

"If that's what you think," the Old Man said bitterly to his only friend, "then you'd best take yours and get."

Parkinson didn't move. In the shadows of the cool room, he looked like an ogre exuding

77

sweat. His darting black eyes with their scaly whites, flecked and mud-shadowed, fell upon his youngest daughter, kneeling by the Old Man's youngest son. There was a ridge of white above the slash of Parkinson's mouth. He hadn't forgotten that she'd run away. Now, they were talking low; the 'breed couldn't hear them.

Carl said: "It's hopeless, Ellie. I shouldn't have stayed. We should've ridden on, just us two."

"That's done, Carl. That's past and over. We've got to think of *now*. Listen to me; it's not too late. I can smell the blood that's going to splash these walls. If we don't get up and go right now, we'll never be able to leave. We'll die here." She twisted the cloth of his shirt-sleeve. "Come on, Carl . . ."

While they argued, Matthew looked at Judith Anne, saying nothing. They weren't close now. In this situation they had no common ground, like down in the breaks along the creek. *There*, they had familiarity, lust; here there was nothing to bind them close. So he just looked at her, long-legged, jet-hair caught up behind with a ribbon, lips parted, returning his stare out of an intent and watchful face.

Kid Marcy leaned against the cool wall and looked from one to the other and kept up his frayed smile. *These people are crazy; downright*

78

*crazy, if they think they can stand off much of a
posse for long, in here. But I'm a little crazy, too,
and that old man's got something I want to see
more of. I'll stay yet a while . . .*

"We ought to," Carl said. "We ought to,
Ellie; just get up from here and walk out, go
away; that's what we *ought* to do."

"Come on, then."

"God knows, I want to. I don't hate anyone
bad enough to want to kill them. I don't want
to fight those people—be hated all the time.
You know what I want."

"Yes, I know."

"But I can't, Ellie. You know that, too."

She still knelt beside him. Now she sunk
lower, sitting back on her heels and the intentness died out of her face leaving an ugly
stoicism that seemed to broaden, flatten, her
features, Fortunately, Carl didn't notice or he
might have been struck by her Indianness;
been repelled by the fatalism and coarseness.
He wasn't looking at her.

From the doorway, Kid Marcy called out.
"You got plenty of water in here—Jacob?
Plenty of ammunition and food?"

With the quaking diminishing in his hands,
but without turning, Jacob said, "We've got
enough to stand a long siege, don't worry.
This ain't the first time this house has been
'seiged."

79

"But it might be the last time," the Kid said, genuinely amused, pale eyes sparkling.

The Old Man got crimson in the face and flung around. "I told you," he thundered, "if you're scairt, to on—ride off. There's still plenty of time."

The Kid glanced around without replying and grim humour lingered on his face. Then he slouched forward again, resuming his vigil. Judith Anne sidled closer to Matthew.

"Who is he?"

"Kid Marcy, a gunman. He broke out of jail with us."

"He's little," Judith Anne said, who was long and lithe. She appraised Marcy carefully. "My hands are bigger'n his. Graceful, ain't he?"

Matthew gazed at her, mumbled something and went over where John Parkinson was laying out brass cartridges, with wooden-faced reserve. As Matthew began plugging gaps in his shell-belt the 'breed spoke to the Old Man again.

"They'll out-wait you, Jacob."

"I think not. They won't stay out in that sun for long without water. The well's too close to the house for them to get any there."

"They'll bring water."

"Not enough for a seige. For a day, maybe; two days."

John Parkinson went back to lining up the casings in neat rows. He was silent, but frowning.

The Old Man wasn't thinking of the battle, of the seige. He'd thought that out years before, when he'd built the house with a view to standing off redskins and renegades from within it. When he'd worried up each great stone of the walls, dug the well close by, scooped out a deep, narrow cellar to hide in as a last resort, made it a secret place.

He thought of Oklahoma; place for a free life away from Bloody Kansas and Missourian night-riders, from Yankee and Secesh. A place with a kind of climate where men minded their own affairs and survived. Where they worked with their hands and created something of nothing. *Christ in Heaven, what a lie!* Remembered years blurred with pain and toil and ache.

Oklahoma! Hell-heat summers, drought, cracked earth, hunger and want; renegades and redskins in droves. Sunshine as red as blood, as dry as tinder. Every winter a scourge, an abomination filled with croup and colic, with distempers of all kinds and with marrow so frozen, you could hardly unbend your fingers for days at a time. With sickness coming in around the rattling doors, poisons in the frigid white frost.

And the war reaching down this far. The clatter of soldiers riding, looting, plundering, burning. Of taking refuge in the stone house until they'd gone, then peering out at empty corrals. At dust high over driven livestock and the spectre of starvation close.

And retaliating, striking back, fighting tooth and fang for survival and raising the young in that image. Of coming through lean and wild, but surviving where others left, or died, or became lawless, which was understandable, but also became godless, which was not.

And now this—being deserted by the woman of his flesh. A floodtide of harshness bursting past a dam in his mind. Wrongs he'd known were wrongs and yet had also known they'd been necessary. But she'd never forgot them; they'd lived in her, growing, until now—this.

And the obscure god in his brain that cried out things in the thunderous silence had wrung him limp. So that he longed to scream at the top of his lungs to them all—in this room and beyond it—fight! Fight and survive, it was all that mattered!

"Paw?"

He knew the deep, but timorous voice and stiffened his mind against it, for of them all still alive, Carl was most like *her* with his gentleness, his want, his need for things to come to life under his hands, and *she* had deserted him.

"Paw; listen to me. We can't lick 'em *all.*"

The words quivered in the stillness and exploded inside the Old Man's head. It was in him too; this one which was most like her. He would run out, too.

The Old Man looked around, white-faced, terrible to see with the sunken eyes flaming in a deadly way. He wasn't a cursing man, but he could curse and now he did. Carl braced into the force of his fury, pale and awed.

Matthew lingered, watching, and when he started across the room he was too late. The Old Man lashed out, struck downward with his bony fist, and Carl crumpled, then Matthew was between them, leaning into the Old Man's weight, being sprayed with sour spittle.

"I know what I'm doing! If you're a coward, you can go. God knows this room, big as it is, ain't big enough for a coward. In the end *she* broke. In the end you will too, but I cannot—Matthew . . . cannot!"

When the Old Man's weight drew back, shaking, Matthew bent, grasped Carl and helped him up. Behind the youngest son, Ellie stood, round and handsome, dusky and big-eyed, paler than Matthew had ever seen her before. It flashed in Matthew's mind that Ellie really, sincerely, loved his brother. And that was ironic.

"Turn him out!" the Old Man ordered.

Matthew ignored him, guided Carl back across the room to the little bench. Ellie trailed them.

"Sinner!" the Old Man called out.

"Matthew . . . He's *crazy*. He's going to get us all killed in here. Can't you see that?"

"Sit down, Carl. There's something I see you don't. If we break out of here and go off separately, they'll get us one at a time, like shooting crows. If it's to be a finish-fight, it's better this way. All together. After we broke out of their jail they'll have the whole damned countryside stirred up."

Ellie touched Matthew's sleeve. "But if we *all* left; all together, we'd have strength and still be able to move around. This way we're just—"

"It's too late, Ellie."

"Except for *him* it wouldn't be."

Carl sank down and Matthew stood above him. There was a puffiness to the younger brother's cheek where the Old Man's fist had struck. Ellie went down on her heels and Matthew watched her. Could the same depth of feeling be in Judith Anne? He turned to look at the older girl.

Judith Anne was over by the door smiling down at Kid Marcy.

So the day wore on; with the Old Man putting everything in shape for a hard battle and muttering to himself, sunken eyes burning with a strange obsession. John Parkinson groping to fathom his own feelings, his reluctance to stay, yet shrinking away from the scorn if he tried to leave. And as always, because his mind was cramped-tight and slow, arriving at no decision.

With Carl and Ellie inert, held close by a bond of futility. Silent, waiting, drowning in despair and tainted with bitterness.

With Judith Anne fascinated by the diminutive, wispy gunman. Bending to adjust a spur that needed no adjusting knowing the Kid could look down and see the richness of her flesh swelling ripe and full above the slackness of her blouse.

With Matthew in a turmoil, filled with dying hopes and disillusionment, wondering half-heartedly if they would live *this* one out. Refusing to look at Judith Anne; not hating the Kid, but pitying him.

With the sun sliding off the meridian, slanting its froth of shimmering heat over everything until there were no shadows, no depths, only angles and lines and blinding brightness. And silence.

The wearing stillness, the eternal hush of naked land eating at their nerves until the men wished with all their might *something* would happen; anything at all to break the stagnancy, the bondage of thought, of memory, of wonder, which was beginning to warp their spirits and dissolve their wills.

The Kid finally turned his head from Judith Anne with a high ruddy flush, and grew subtly still with erect watchfulness, staring straight out. Slim, almost woman-like in his grace and wispiness, the dark sheen of shellbelt and holster looking out of place around his small waist. The sweep of his walnut-butted revolver artistically swooping in its ominous way.

And in the utter quiet of the stone house, his words fell soft and pleasant, carelessly spoken, velvet in depth and meaning.

"Riders coming from the west. I reckon the wait is over . . ."

CHAPTER FOUR

The Kid stood just inside the door looking out into the stark brilliance, pale eyes drawn low and narrow. A sound of horsemen came clearly through the stillness. Old Man

Fenwick crossed the room with big strides, ducked his head and squinted out.

No one spoke nor scarcely moved. John Parkinson's face grew iron-like. Carl straightened a little on the bench, flinging back his wide shoulders. Ellie was still and apathetic. Matthew poked wadding from a loophole in the wall and waited, while Judith Anne watched the old man's long, wide back.

"How many do you make out?" the Old man asked Kid Marcy.

"Fifteen."

"That's right." The Old Man stepped back and looked at the others. "Fifteen," he said in a ringing way. "Seven of us behind stone walls and the only water's right here—ten feet from the house. They won't get us!"

John Parkinson picked up a rifle with reluctance, went to a loophole and snatched away the greased rag. A round ferrule of sunlight jumped through. His leather-like face was wreathed with sweat.

Kid Marcy waited until the possemen drew up, out a ways, talking among themselves, then he eased the door nearly closed, approved its great oaken thickness, the oversizedness of its sheath-hinges and wrought hardware. Nothing short of a howitzer could demolish it.

The Old Man snatched up a rifle and ges-

87

tured with it like Joshua outside The Walls. "Get to the loopholes," he said. "Don't fire-off 'till I say, and remember this—*kill their horses!*" His eyes watched them move into position, but his mind—his sight—said there was one who might not obey him so he went up beside Kid Marcy and glared downwards. "Do like I say—only the horses. In here I'm captain—remember that."

The Kid nodded. There was almost a frightening compulsion to the strange, wild eyes. "The horses," he repeated, and slid sideways with a rifle, knelt by the crack in the door and watched the possemen start riding again, closer, up towards the yard. Then they stopped and a man with a spade-beard rode apart and the Kid knew him; Sheriff Bunsen. He hooked one hand around the edge of the door until the knuckles were white, laid the musket across it and drew the target down the barrel to his eyes, and waited.

"You there! Fenwick . . . Come outside!"

The Old Man straightened up, listening, his mouth flat in its wonted slit and a secret fierce joy singing within him. "Open it wider," he said to the Kid, and filled the opening with his breadth, the rifle held low in both hands, ready.

"I'm here," the Old Man boomed. "Take

your settlement scum out'n my yard!"

"You old fool," Bunsen said in his hard way, "if you don't put down that gun you'll be dead before sundown."

"Not alone, I won't be," the Old Man thundered. "We had nothing to do with killing Will Parson, but we ain't going to be judged by *your* kind of law, either. Now get!"

"Fenwick . . . !"

"I won't argue. I mean for you to get. If you don't, I'll *make* you."

Bunsen sat in dark-brooding stillness, his beard glowing with rich sunlight. Behind him, well back, the Old Man saw Harry Cumberland. There were others he recognised, too. Then Bunsen turned his horse, rode back and began gesturing with his arm to the possemen. The Old Man watched them ride off a ways, fan out as though to surround the house and he stepped back, closed the door and dropped the bar. There was a red flush of excitement to him.

"Now," he said, "before they get beyond range. Just the horses!"

John Parkinson fired first. The puff of powder blew outward and the explosion stung his ears. Bunsen's horse gave a mighty leap and folded under the sheriff. Men screamed. Carl fired and stepped back to reload. Ellie moved in with dull-eyed certainty, using the same loophole. The stone house blossomed grey smoke. Matthew had a loophole to himself. Judith Anne used one farther down the room, closer to Kid Marcy.

The Old Man's shirt darkened with sweat, his eyes ran tears from the searing fumes of black powder and beyond the house men were yelling, spurring to get away from the senselessness Pete Bunsen had led them into, for the fire from the stone house was far greater than it was supposed to be, and dead-accurate; so accurate the ugly house was wreathed in smoke and there were dead horses everywhere and Pete Bunsen was stunned with the rapidity of his defeat. Three of his fifteen men were lying still near their dead horses while two more, pinned under threshing animals, yelled for help, which none dared give them and the rest of the men were flying every which way.

Bunsen howled for the men to drop—get down. By then, the crashing gunfire from the house was dwindling and there wasn't a single horse left standing. A man lying pressed-flat near the sheriff raised his head.

"How many's in there, Pete? You said there was only them three and Kid Marcy."

"I don't know. I got no idea—what happened. They got friends with 'em. Christ, we can't stay like this—they'll pick us off like stoning crows."

"The barn," the man said.

Bunsen yelled for his men to make for the barn. Some had already run too far out to hear him, thinking only to get beyond rifle range. Others were afraid to get up off the ground. Others leapt up and raced for it. Harry Cumberland and Pete Bunsen among them.

Inside the house, the Old Man leaned his rifle against the wall. "Anybody hurt?" There were headshakes, no words. "Now see how the tide's turnt," he said. "They're 'sieged, we ain't. We can hold 'em in that barn as long as we want.

"Until nightfall," Matthew said shortly. "They'll slip away in the dark and you know it."

"Not if we don't want 'em to, they won't."

Matthew turned, laid aside his musket and wiped sweat off his face with a shirtsleeve. "What sense is there to keepin' 'em in there?" he said.

"Gain time, boy. To gain time," the Old Man told him. "When we break out of here we'll want lots of time to make tracks."

Kid Marcy twisted his head away from the slit by the door. He alone among them was still holding his gun, still kneeling and watchful. "We *had* time this morning. I told you that."

91

"You tell me nothing," the Old Man roared at him. "I'm captain here. I been through more sieges right here in this house than you've ever heard of. This morning we had four, five hours. What we need is days; you remember that."

The Kid moved his eyes to Judith Anne. She was watching Ellie and Carl who were standing together in dull silence.

"Tonight we leave."

"Afoot?" Kid Marcy said, incredulously. "We shot all . . ."

"Shut up, you!"

The silence drew out until the Old Man willed it broken, then he spoke again. "Tonight two of us'll stay here; keep them tied down in the barn. The rest of us'll go to John Parkinson's, get horses and ride."

Matthew was looking hard at the Old Man. "Which two?" he asked thinly.

The Old Man's wild glare became narrow and cruel. "Carl for one," he said. That and no more.

They all looked across the room. Ellie was staring blackly at the Old Man. Carl's gaze was low, along the floor. His mouth was partly open. Big shoulders sagged.

Ellie said, "You know who the other one'll be, don't you?"

When the Old Man said nothing, showed

only cold triumph in his expression, John Parkinson came heavily forward. "Not you, Ellie," he said. "One woman's gone—that's enough."

There was the stillness again, thickening, settling. The Old Man still wore his expression of knowing triumph. "Come tomorrow," he said, "when you can't hold 'em any longer, Carl, you'll hide in the secret cellar . . . you and whoever stays with you. They'll ransack the place, but they'll never find you. After they've gone—afoot—you make it to Parkinson's. We'll leave horses there aplenty. Take to the breaks down Chagrin Creek and track us. We'll have better'n two days start that way. You understand?"

"I understand."

"*We* understand," Ellie said.

Her father looked black and doubting, but there was no time, for the attackers were firing again. Long, spaced shots put where they might find a way inside. The defenders turned back to their task, returning the fire just as blindly.

It went like that until the blazing sun slid off down the tattered sky, bullets making a flat, ripping sound against the stone. Farther out, where the barn was, bullets tore long grooves through the wood, rattling inside the barn among Bunsen and his men there, until darkness came.

The Old Man ordered Matthew to make up bundles of food. They had one lamp going in a corner of the room on the floor. It cast monstrous, hideously mis-shapen shadows up along the oak-runnered ceiling. Only metal sparkled dully. Metal, and their eyes, which probed everywhere. Parkinson talked to Ellie aside, but she was adamant, pale as a ghost and deadly afraid, but unmovable in her determination.

"Well, then," the 'breed said, "I didn't know, girl. That's why you run off to him in the settlement?"

"Yes."

"But Christ a'mighty, Ellie . . . you want to *live* with him, not *die* with him!"

"You *knew*," she said, "but you didn't go away, did you?"

"It's different. I fight. I *like* to fight. It's different."

"This is what I want."

Parkinson looked at her and groped for words, but never found them because he wasn't sure he even knew them and in the moist parts of his brain there'd always been an idea about her and the youngest Fenwick, so he shrugged and went back over by the table where guns and cartridges lay, leaned upon it next to the Old Man. But as he talked, his eyes

94

stayed on Ellie, back beside hulking Carl.

"I can't move her."

"Don't try," the Old Man said with tainted breath.

"She ain't yours . . . "

"*He* is."

"You don't act it, sometimes."

The Old Man's head snapped back. "I raised *men,*" he hissed. "I raised 'em to read sign and melt into shadows and ride like Indians. He'll survive."

Kid Marcy ambled over beside Matthew, watched the big hands stow food into bundles and smiled upwards. "You think it'll work?"

"It'll work," Matthew said. "He knows what he's doing."

Marcy nodded absently, knew Judith Anne was watching him and turned to gaze at her in the shadows, saw how the light fell into the dark places around her, making contrasts. "How far's Parkinson's?" he asked absently.

"About five miles," Matthew said without looking up. "Couple hours trotting time."

Marcy strolled back by the door and Judith Anne's gaze clung to him with a hotness.

The Old Man slipped outside when night was down full black. He was gone twenty minutes and when he returned, there was a quick spring to his step. "Like moles," he said. "They got a man outside watching."

"They'll send someone off to Osage."

The Old Man shook his head. "They already did. I got him from behind."

Carl looked up at his father. "You didn't shoot," he said.

"Clubbed him. Matthew—you about ready?"

"I'm ready."

"Then give them the bundles and let's go."

John Parkinson was last through the door. Ellie had smothered the lamp and there was only the heavy darkness. He lingered a second, looking at her, then he was gone and Carl closed the door and dropped the bar down.

From her crouched position by the lantern, Ellie turned away from him, shielded her face which was drawn and still. "We'd better make sure about the cellar," she said.

Carl moved sluggishly. You had to smooth the dust on the floor to find the little slit that led downward into a stygian, damp-smelling slot of space. When they were through examining it, Ellie was satisfied. She stood up brushing dust off her hands.

"Did anyone ever use it?" she asked.

"Until now, no one ever had to," Carl said. "The Old Man made it in case he'd misfigured—in case someone got inside sometime when we were 'seiged."

"He thinks of everything," she said, and

96

went towards the mess Matthew had left on the table. "Do you want something to eat?"

"I couldn't eat."

She looked at him. "Scairt?"

"Sick."

She went beside him and reached out, "What about tomorrow," she said. "Not the day—our tomorrow?"

"I don't know." He pushed dust with his boot-toe. "I don't think there'll be any."

"There can be . . . If we go now 'stead of waiting."

He scowled at his boot. "That wouldn't do. It'd be betraying them."

"They've got their start. Those men in the barn'll lie low 'till dawn. The most we can do is hold them a couple more hours after sunup. You know that. Then crawl into that little hole like rats. And if we're found down there . . . "

"What do you think's in my mind, anyway?"

"Then let's go right now."

"No, it's wrong and you know it is."

"He's got a hold on you, Carl. On both of you. He's even got a hold on my paw—and that outlaw you brought back from the settlement with you. He's got a hold on all of you." She stiffened with feeling, leaned towards him. "But not on me. I know what he's going to do . . . Get us all killed. Don't let it be. We

97

can get away. We can get to our place, get horses and ride North—not after them—out of the Territory, Carl."

"Ellie . . ."

"You said that's what you want—you know it's what I want, too."

He stood up suddenly and took up his rifle. "I'm going to look around outside."

When he moved towards the door she sprang up and stood stiff, watching him. "Carl . . . don't go out there!"

"I got to. It's close in here. I got to think, Ellie."

"They'll be watching. You heard what he said. They got a man out back of the barn, watching."

"A settlement man," Carl said, lifting the bar. "Close this after me an' if I'm not back shortly, get down in the cellar and stay there."

He left.

The night was soft and benign. It was filled with the rich scent of cooling iron, of dust and oily plants. Carl moved with unconscious stealth, betraying no pleasure at the smells he'd revelled in other times. Of earth and night-life and fragrant coolness.

The barn stood crumpled in shadow, still and ominous. He watched it and listened. They were there, crouched in fear, what was left of them. Knowing they were out-manned

98

by the Fenwicks who'd grown up in this stark country; were one with the night when they chose to be. Could out-Indian the best of them, so they lay close and glued their eyes to the slits in the warped wood and waited for sunup, afraid to venture out.

And he thought of what she'd said. Mostly it was true; the best they could do, come daylight, was hold them off for a couple of hours. By now the Old Man, Matthew, the others, would be saddling up over at Parkinson's. Riding softly down the shadows towards Chagrin Creek, bearing south with stealth and caution. Armed to the teeth and strong.

And what if the possemen found the little hole under the house? They'd hang them both. Maybe worse. What was ahead if they went after the others? There was strength wherever the Old Man was; he'd come to manhood with that in his head. There was strength when the Fenwicks stood together.

He took his pistol and kept it behind him where no stray light might find it and begun stalking the barn. He went far out around the corrals, pale and boney in the darkness, and came down behind the barn scarcely breathing, and saw the darker hunk of something squatting low by a corner of the leached old wood.

He knew it for a man—a foolish man—

when the tiny glow of a sucked-on cigarette winked redly at him. Lying flat on his belly he laid the pistol across his arm, drew steady and fired.

The sentinel leapt straight up in the air. A cascade of tiny sparks scattered from the broken cigarette and the man fell flat and began to wriggle frantically like a terrified snake.

It might do, he thought, edging back out where darkness lay. It might hold them for a while—until sunup. He went back to the house and scratched the door. Ellie let him in. She was so erect her movements were stilted.

"Was that you shot, Carl?"

"Yes. Go make us up a bundle, Ellie. We're going."

"Did you kill one?"

"Shot beside him, into the barn. Hurry up."

She hurried to the table and her hands moved like tethered birds, fighting blindly for release. When she twisted up the cloth, turned, he was looming over her. His face was alive with a ghostly light.

"Can you run beside me?"

"Yes," she said, "you know I can."

"Yes, I know you can . . . You're pretty, Ellie."

She moved around him swiftly, stopped at the door and waited. he peered out. There

100

was a stillness deeper than death over everything.

"Come on—stay close."

They went like phantoms; he, with a great,
shambling gait that was half-walk, half-trot.
She with the strong power of her blood,
darkly enduring, stoically suffering from want
of air, but never slowing until they topped out
the ridge and gazed downwards.

A ramshackle log house snuggled close to
the parched ground. Beyond it, a skeleton of a
barn . . . and a night full of stillness.

She touched his arm and they started down
through the brush. There was a strong smell
of horses and cattle in the stale air and once he
slipped in something soft, caught himself and
plunged on. They drew up in a thicket of grey
sage and remained statue-like until satisfied,
then she went across the yard and he caught
her at the corrals where horses watched them
with drowsy interest.

"Get what you want from the house; I'll
saddle up."

His hands were hot with sweat. The sour-
ness of excitement exuding from him made
the horses snort, roll their eyes and bunch up.
He took two, clamped saddles upon them,
knocked back the bits with a great pad of a
thumb and led the beasts out. She came flying
to him and a pale glow of ground-light limned

her. He watched with a hardness in his throat, handed the reins out mutely and sprang up.

They rolled through the night with a soft thudding of hooves, a dry creaking of leather, a long, thin whistling of breath—southward.

"No! The other way."

His face turned towards her in blurred softness. "We can't . . . We done enough, Ellie. We can't let them go on thinking we're coming to stand by them when we ain't."

Nor would argument sway him. Desperation grew out of her until she caught the acidness of his profile, became silent. After a time he turned towards her.

"We already did less what we were supposed to do." There was that blind allegiance in his look that stilled her. Damned behind her teeth were words of desperation that rang like flutes in her mind. Why must he be so weak? Why must the Old Man have such an iron hold on them all?

"You understand . . . ?"

"I understand," she replied. "I understand a lot better'n you do. He won't let us go."

"We'll go, Ellie." There grew a softness to his voice. "We'll have things right, you'll see."

"I'll see . . ."

The hours slipped by. They swung south along the breaks paralleling the unkempt swathes of willows, tall and graceful in the gloom. Beyond, through the wilderness sedge they saw the creek, all dark-oily and with a pale miasma of cloudiness hanging above it chockful of poisons.

Until his excitement died away and wonderment came in its place, he walked the horse, letting it pick its own way, while the big man upon its back reflected in his brooding way, growing sad gently, sad and wistful—appearing in the face, swaying along gently, lost among a tumbling bramble of thoughts.

It was false-dawn before either of them spoke, then it was Ellie, whose sharp black glance picked up sign. She pointed to it.

"There—near the creek, Carl. Tracks."

He looked. "Water's still seeping in. They can't be more'n a few miles ahead."

"You won't branch off?"

"I can't."

The sun came up an hour later. A gigantic smouldering disc of it all pale and swollen looking. Heat came shortly after. Shadows scampered back under things, hunkered there in terror. The land glowed for another hour, warmly benevolent, until gradually the fury came sucking at the air's freshness, making it sour and oppressive. By then they had seen the faint twisting of transparent dust far ahead and off to their right. Carl watched it with troubled wonder. The Old Man was surcease—he was also oppression. He twisted a little in his saddle to look at Ellie. He marvelled that after what had gone forward those past hours she could still look clean and cool. The fullness of her, full-length, still had resiliency to it.

"We made good time."

"Yes," she said, but tonelessly and her gaze was fixed on the distant dustcloud.

"What is it, Ellie?"

"I don't know. A fright, I reckon."

He turned quickly and stared hard towards the dust. Internal hackles arose, stood bristling a second, then dwindled away and he scowled over at her. "It's them," he said.

"Is it? How can you tell?"

"It's about where they'll be. You saw the . . . "

"I got a notion, Carl. Chagrin Creek's turning southeast down here. It's been curving for the last couple of hours. If it don't make a sharp cut-back, westward, then that dustcloud might be others."

He puckered up his brows in wonderment, but the fear didn't return so he felt irritated by what she'd said.

"Who else'd be riding so early?"

"I don't know; Indians maybe."

He gripped the reins tighter and locked his jaws tight. After a moment of staring he jerked his head towards the profusion of willows. "Ride down in there. We'll be less likely to make dust."

They wound in and out of the willows with branches snapping back viciously to sting their faces, their bodies, the horses they rode, until the foetid breath of the creek drove them farther out, then Carl said, "I'll take a look. You wait here."

"We'll both go," she said, and rode on past him so that he had no chance to argue.

The land sloped gently away from them in a long roll of whispering grass that broke and swirled upwards as they went through it. There was no cover away from the creek, so Carl was prudent. Before they were separated from the shadows, all tangled and frowsy from the willows, he reined up and stood in the stirrups to see.

It wasn't the Old Man, he knew that, but neither was it hostiles, for there was far too much dust raised. He frowned in an effort to understand. It was movement, he could see that much.

"Can you see them?"

"Yes, but they're too far off to make them out."

"Indians?"

"No, looks to be wagons, maybe, or else a big party of riders."

"Not ours?"

"Too many," he said, straining harder. Then he grunted and dropped back, puzzled. "I'll go closer."

Without speaking she urged her horse out. They rode close together for a half mile then she drew up and he stood in the stirrups again. Watching his sweaty face, she saw the quick rush of consternation.

"What is it?"

"It's riders. They're coming up along the creek, Ellie . . . like they're tracking . . ."

Horror made her sick for a blinding flash, then she swung her horse. "Back up the creek to the ridge we passed. There are trees up there."

He loped after her, twisting from time to time to see the riders. Terror, for the first time he could remember, flooded him. He was alone. Then bitterness, for surely the others had seen the riders, had scouted them up and knew what they were doing. Realisation was slow coming. The Old Man knew. He had schemed it out in his mind. The riders wouldn't find Carl and Ellie, because they'd still be at the stone house; they wouldn't be riding down the creek until long after the riders had swept by. In deserting their post, he and Ellie had ridden into peril and the others wouldn't know it.

106

He wanted to spur up the long slope, fling himself off in the brush and hold the horse's nose until they went past. Instead he rode the loose lope behind Ellie and grew oily in his clothes with fright.

She cut into the first clump of trees where blessed shade lay. She sat stiffly upright in the saddle, her black hair loose and trembling against her shoulders.

"I see them now."

"On both sides of the creek," he said. "We can't stay here; they'll, pick up our sign where we turned back."

"Who can be they be?"

"It don't matter, we can't stay here." Then he remembered what Kid Marcy had said. "Keep moving . . ."

"Wait, Carl. It couldn't be a posse, could it?"

"Look how they're working the willows, riding slow and all bent over. I don't know how—but they're after us, Ellie."

"Cattle? Could they be looking for cattle along the creek?"

"You know better. Only cattle in here are your's and mine—John's and the Old Man's."

"Then the Old Man didn't get their messenger—those men in the barn. Maybe he only thought he did; maybe there was more'n one got out."

107

He grew impatient. "Go east through the trees, Ellie. They'll cut our sign pretty quick. We'll need all the time we can get."

"But why didn't they follow the other tracks?"

He touched the horse lightly with his spurs and edged past her. "I don't know. Right now, I don't care."

They hadn't gone five hundred yards before someone fired a pistol. Carl swung quickly. The possemen were converging on two men standing beside their mounts. The tracks where they'd cut back had been found, fresh and spongy. Even while he watched the big band of horsemen began whirling their mounts in an angling way so as to approach the ridge where the fugitives were, in a wide-spaced line.

"Carl . . . !"

"I see," he said and dug in the spurs.

They rode hard, but in the blistering heat a horse couldn't stand running for long, so they had to slow to a jog for miles on end before they dared push the animals further. It was torture.

There was no sign of the pursuit, but there was no longer any doubt but that it was pursuit, either, so they forged ahead into the cauldron-heat, dry-hot with desperation. When the covert petered out into broken hill-ocks and patchy sage, Carl rode due south and didn't look back until he heard Ellie gasp. She was all beaded with sweat, eyes closed so tightly, water was squeezed out around them.

"What is it?"

"I'm sick."

"Oh, God, you can't be. If we can hold south until afternoon, we'll find the others."

"Keep going," she said without opening her eyes.

Down the lemon-yellow furnace of land until the horses began to lag, Ellie reeling from time to time, both hands locked around the saddlehorn, reins looped and flopping, her horse following Carl's in blind subservience, until far back, dark motes against the dry-tan grass, the shrunken, leached old sky, the possemen were visible. They were far enough back that Carl dared halt briefly. He reined up beside her, reached for her arm and shook it a little.

"Just keep going," she said, without opening her eyes or unlocking her teeth. "It's got to be soon, Carl."

"I don't want to leave you, Ellie."

"You can't leave me." Her eyes flew open; they were half rational, half swimming in agony.

"I won't," he said softly.

They began the gradual descent again, only slower, for they were well beyond rifle range

109

and the possemen were going slower too, as though content for the time being to keep the fugitives in sight, not trying to overhaul them.

Far ahead he saw something shimmering and thought it was his eyes creating hope from the dazzling void. But it didn't lose shape, although it was dark and small, like bunched-up riders going away from him.

He didn't know how hard he was riding the horse until he heard Ellie's horse falter and seconds later the soft thump when she fell.

"Ellie! Ellie, for God's sake, get up!"

He knelt with the reins in his left hand slapping her face. Sweat fell from his chin onto her blouse, staining it with darkness.

"Ellie . . ."

The soft strident yell came gently.

He jumped up and saw them. There was a sharp glitter of guns far back where they were riding down-land. The cry was repeated. They had seen him standing over her beside the horses and although they didn't know why it was so, they knew it was victory for them.

"Go on, Carl . . ."

She was gazing upwards in the shade of his right leg and her underlip bled where she'd bitten through it. She didn't look pretty to him now. She looked sag-muscle-ugly with a sheen of sweat.

"No."

"You must."

He knelt swiftly turning his back upon the long line of fanned-out horsemen. "I'll carry you."

"The horses are done in. You couldn't make it packing me. Go on—catch up with the others." There was dead grass caught in her hair, a strange lustre in her eyes. "Go on, Carl, hurry."

He slid big arms under her, heaved upright, and his heart beat to bursting from the strain, but she was strangely light in his arms and stared blindly into his face until a great welter of tears broke and ran down her face.

He got into the saddle someway, and urged the horse out. Her animal straggled along. There was futility in it. Even in her semi-conscious state, Ellie knew it if he did not.

It was the flat sound of a rifle that brought him to reason. They were coming up fast. He was well within gun range now and the horse laboured under him, stumbled frequently and sucked in air like wind whistling around a too-small hole.

Her head hung slack. He saw the great staunchness of her in his dimming heart and choked over words that rattled in his throat. The horse fell heavily, almost with a sigh, and it was over.

He sat up and cradled her head in his lap.

111

There was a pulsing of blood from one ear. The stickiness ran under his collar and mingled with sweat.

The first horseman yanked back with one hand and levelled a dragon pistol with the other. His face was burnt red-brown around the graceful sweep of a curling moustache. Carl looked up at him and never once considered the pistol at his side, under the ebony strands of Ellie's hair.

"Get up, damn you! Stand up!"

"I can't."

The big pistol wavered, sagged a little as others droned up and stopped, peering downwards.

"Are you hurt?"

"No," he touched Ellie's face with his fingers, "she is."

"Leave her be and stand up."

He saw them dismount and scatter out around him. Their faces were flushed and hard. So he put her head gently in the grass and stood heavily upright.

"Throw down that pistol."

He discarded it, looking at them with a sickness of his own, down deep—a sense of guilt and failure.

"There's plenty of trees back up that ridge," a thin man said.

There were others who echoed it until the

storm grew around him. Then a man in a rusty, black hat, whose eyes were hidden behind folds of perpetually puckered flesh, pushed up close and stared at Carl.

"Where's the others was in the stone house with you?"

"Gone, I don't know where."

"Yes, you do," the older man said flintily. "You know all right."

"Hang the subbitch."

"Better'n that—shoot him right here."

"Shut up, dammit! Now then—don't lie to me, Fenwick. Where's your old man and them others with him?"

"I'm not lying. I don't know."

The puckered eyes went to Ellie, lingered there a moment. "You two split off, did you? It don't matter, we'll catch 'em. Every damned one of them." The eyes dropped away again. "What's ailing her?"

"She said she was sick then she fell off the horse. I don't know."

The man knelt, laid a coarse hand upon Ellie's face. Behind him, the voices began again. He ignored them, arose finally and looked hard at Carl.

"One's better'n none," he said. "Don't fear, we'll get the others. This is good enough to start with."

" . . . Back to the oaks. We'll leave his car-

113

case swinging and twistin' up there for all to see."

The puckered eyes were savage behind their slits, and as cold as death, but they weren't brutal eyes. The man waved a hand downward.

"And what'll y'do with her; leave her here, y'goddamned blabbermouths?"

"She's no better or she wouldn't be with 'im."

"Maybe not," the man said, "but what of her young?"

There was a sucked-in silence. "Didn't think of that, did you? She's with child—maybe you want to strangle that, too."

Carl shook with a hard, brittle quivering and his eyes bulged.

"No," he said, "no, she don't have any such thing. You're crazy."

"Like your old man's crazy?" There were several cold headshakes. "No, I'm not. I raised three daughters, Fenwick. Think I don't know what ails 'em like this? Well, I do. She's with young, an' if you don't know it, you ought to be horsewhipped."

CHAPTER FIVE

Matthew knelt deep in the tangled muck among the willows far southward along Chagrin Creek. The Old Man was there with him, moving softly and muttering. Back a ways, on dryer ground, John Parkinson munched food and watched the horses eat. Judith Anne lay in the coolness of early evening with her eyes closed, exhausted and parched feeling.

They waited in the soft green light of dying day, hardly speaking, moving sluggishly when they moved at all, for they were weary. An immensity of quietude weighed down upon them.

The Old Man leapt up and spoke in a low, harsh tone. "What's keeping them, anyway?"

"Maybe they got caught," Matthew said. "Maybe they got found in the cellar."

"I don't believe that; no, I don't believe that at all. A sight of cunning went into making that hole, Matthew." There was almost pleading to the way the Old Man said it.

"Then what else could it be?" Matthew said irritably. "They had plenty of time."

"The heat," his father said quickly. "They had to favour their horses because of the cursed heat."

Matthew made a soft scorning sound and kept his vigil. Night birds, mostly owls, skimmed silently through the darkness of the shadows, a whisper of a sound, gentle and deadly. Later, there was something louder; a faint crackling, a snapping. There was movement up the creek a ways, where the deep-dyed night lay thickest. John Parkinson's jaw froze to stillness. Judith Anne opened her black eyes and listened. They were fearful, but steeled. The sound came closer—the crashing of something through the willows and finally a muted call, soft and silky with caution. It came again and Matthew got heavily upright and leaned on his rifle.

"It's the Kid come back," he said.

The Old Man was rooted, pangs of doubt, of wonderment and apprehension wrenching at him. "Go see what he found."

Matthew went, huge and silent, trailing his musket. When he saw the horseman moving through the blackness he made a night-bird sound and the Kid altered his course, drew up and peered downward.

"I went as far as I dared," he said.

"You didn't find them?"

"Nothing but a dead horse."

"What? Saddled?"

Marcy bobbed his head watching pale light

116

wash the upturned face. "It was one of theirs, I'll bet on that. I recognised the saddle as one we left behind at Parkinson's."

"Oh, Christ!" Matthew flung away, but the Kid's voice called him back.

"Hold on. The other horse was gone. They'd have two."

"What of it? How far could they both go on one horse, you fool? They've been taken."

"No," the Kid said, "not unless they left the house last night they haven't been. You saw that posse from the south. They'd have got to the house before Carl and Ellie left."

"Who else'd be using the saddle you saw? It's them; sure as God made green apples, it was them, and they been taken."

The stinking mist was rising over the creek-water when Matthew crashed past willows and fetched up, facing the Old Man.

"Well?"

"They been taken."

"What?"

"They been taken." He stumbled past, towards Judith Anne and John Parkinson. "Ask the Kid. He found a dead horse."

John Parkinson reached out with a curled fist and pulled Matthew up close. His eyes were questioning.

The Old Man stalked unheedingly through the willows, out where the Kid was walking

117

beside his horse. Stopped before the smaller man, drawn up and craggy. "Are you sure it was them?" he asked.

"Who else would be using Parkinson's saddle," the Kid said, and moved on by leading his horse.

The Old Man fell in beside him. "Tell me," he said. The Kid told him what he'd found. When he was finished the Old Man scowled.

"No blood? No signs of a fight?"

"It was gettin' late. I couldn't see too well, but I didn't see any sign of a scrap."

"What happened to the horse?"

"A bullet."

The Old Man moved quickly. Taloned fingers closed around the Kid's arm, jerked and ground down like steel. "There was a fight then, damn you."

"Let go my arm, Fenwick."

The Old Man 's hand dropped away, hung knotted at his side.

"I told you it was hard to read sign, getting dark an' all. If it was a fight it was over damned soon. I crouched down close, Fenwick. The grass wasn't mussed up much and there wasn't no blood."

The Old Man searched the thin, pinched face with his smouldering stare, then he moved back where the others were and left Marcy to hobble his horse and off-saddle.

Matthew watched him drop down on the warm ground. There was bitterness in his face, but he said nothing. John Parkinson was squatting, eating again, as silent and still as the Indian he really looked like.

Judith Anne swung to look at the Old Man's back. There was feline loathing in her eyes. A soundless, searing hatred that had never been there before. She had never liked the Old Man—who did?—but until now it had been distaste; distaste tinted, maybe, with a thin edging of fear and uneasiness because he was strange—but it was hatred now. What had the old madman let happen to her sister? And Paw . . . She looked at John Parkinson hunched over, chewing like a patient cow. Cold-blooded 'breed . . .

"Ilow did thcy happcn to be down this far, Paw?"

"Who?"

"Dammit, you know who I mean—that posse. How did they get so far south they cussed near cut us off?"

"How would I know?" the Old Man hissed wrathfully. But he knew . . . He hadn't caught the only runner . . . There had been another. Someone who fled after the first firing. Run all the way back to Osage and from there word had gone out. Men had taken to saddle. If this last posse was so far south, by now the land was swarming with posses. He ground his teeth in despair, imagined himself flinging upright, screaming for them all to get to horse, to ride and save themselves. But when his gaze cleared and focused, he was still sitting there, all hunched over, a big, gaunt old buzzard of a man.

"Now what?" Matthew demanded, and the Old Man glared upwards at him with fierce annoyance, aware that Judith Anne, Kid Marcy, even 'breed John, were looking at him closely.

"We got to think," he said.

Judith Anne made a sound. "*We!*" she said.

The Old Man looked swiftly at her. Thick dark hair hung past her shoulders, loosened from the ribbon, and her face showed strangely golden in the murk. He was thinking swiftly; "She is evil, maybe worse than her sister. Ellie led Carl to doom, this one will lead Matthew. No, she won't. I'll see to that. And she's trouble; she's trouble for me, for Matthew. She's trouble for Marcy, too; I've seen that from the edge of my eye. But I need John, so I got to keep her."

"We got to rest," he said finally, "and eat. The horses need rest, too."

He puttered around the soiled bundles, found food and forced it down. The others sat silently still, bulging shapes in the night, for there could be no fire. Mosquitoes came so bad they were finally forced away from the creek, out onto the plain where the horses were. John Parkinson stomped down grass, laid upon it and slept. Judith Anne felt the Kid drop down beside her in a supposedly careless fashion. It didn't fool her.

When Matthew left, walked out to the horses to be alone with his bitterness, the Kid put a hand on her. She shook it off and spoke in a twisted, soft way.

"Don't!"

He lay back then, not angry, and watched the miserly little stars flicker. There was more patience in him than any of the others possessed. He would wait.

When John Parkinson awoke, began fluffing dead grass from his hair, the new day wasn't far off. "We can't stay here," he said suddenly to the Old Man's back. "If that posse's out there'll be others, Jacob."

"I know," the hunched up figure said quietly. "They'll hunt every corner for us now."

"Let's light out."

"They'll be northward, too," the Old Man went on, for Kid Marcy's benefit. "The 'Nation'll be closed to us."

"If we can get down into Texas ..." Parkinson said.

"Not Texas, John. They'll have the Rangers

121

roused up, too."

Matthew was back in the shadows. He'd been listening. Now he said, "All right; you've told us all that's bad—now tell us what's *good* to do."

The Old Man looked around at him in a squinting way. "We got to hide for a few days. We got to lie close."

"Close?"

"In country we know every inch of."

Matthew stared and John Parkinson stopped patting grass from his hair and Kid Marcy rose up on one elbow.

"There's places back on our own range, I know. There's places I've hid things in years gone by, where we could hide out for a long time and no posse would ever find us."

Marcy looked from the Old Man to Parkinson, then to Matthew. The 'breed spoke first. "I don't know, Jacob . . ."

The Old Man flung out an arm, gestured angrily with it to the points of the compass. "They're out all over the land. You know that! The farther south we go the less we know the country—the better others know it. If we stay close—in our own territory—I defy any man, red or white, to catch us off guard."

So they broke camp and rode back with fragrant coolness pleasuring their senses, although they heeded it not. Moving carefully up the odorous bendings of Chagrin Creek, they were well within land all but Marcy knew. They rode furtively, five phantoms on dumb brutes, whose hides showed milky where dried sweat was salt-chalky.

At last they broke out into the crumpled land of swift rises and falls where scrub-oak clumps and sage grew, and thudded over the countryside in a swift mass towards secret places. Even Judith Anne's eyes shone with craftiness now, for here at least, the elements were their allies.

The wan crack of daylight found them loping through an upland where underbrush grew thick and spiny. Where trees rose straight on spindly trunks and where choked creeks ran below the sage and hummock-grass and wild berries.

The Old Man stopped on a razorbacked ridge with John Parkinson beside him. "There," he said triumphantly, throwing out an arm, "There's the cave no one can approach without being seen for miles.

He was right and the others knew it, all but Kid Marcy, who looked over with admiration at the sloping hill that arose above the cavern. The only way a man couldn't see from in there was eastward, and he thought it would be no job to put a guard atop the hill for that.

They set up their camp and beat out trails

123

through the wirey brush to the creek and around the side of the hill to the overhead lip where Kid Marcy sat by the hour, watching, pleasantly occupied with making a rawhide rope from strips he'd cut in a circular way from green hides of a deer. The days throbbed on, as hot as ever, as dazzling-bright and leaching. But there was no suffering, no discomfort. They came to relax, to perk up and look at one another. Only the Old Man seemed unaffected by the peacefulness—the whiling hours. Externally he seemed unaffected because he remained taciturn, as hard and unbending as ever. What went on inside him, none of them knew, but they would find out—they would find out.

Marcy squatted on the perch he'd made overhead and lolled in the shade of a scrubby old tree with his rifle leaning close, his pistol sagging low, unheeded at his hip. He commanded a view for many shimmering miles and day after day there was no movement, nothing to see. Occasionally, a deer would step across his vision, light-footed and graceful. If they were in need of meat he'd call softly down to John, who would snatch up his gun and go out. Otherwise, the Kid kept his peaceful vigil and thought his odd thoughts and was undisturbed until the sparkling forenoon Judith Anne came to him up there.

She smiled in a restless way until he invited her into the shade where she sank down.

"You can see almost to the settlement from here, can't you?"

Watching her profile, seeing how the hair-line grew down almost to her temples, he nodded. There was the look of a torpid serpent to him—the look of indomitable patience rewarded.

"Almost." He drew up off the ground and leaned forward. "Once I saw Indians over near that bosque there . . . " His breath touched her neck and down along her shoulder.

Her nostrils quivered while her eyes stayed far out in a soft-thrilled way. She knew he was looking down, but she made no move to draw back. There was that tickling. Besides, Matthew had grown apart from her of late. Not that it mattered. There had been a time, but that was gone and long ago.

"I found arrow-points up here. Indians must've used this place for years," he said smoothing the dust near her hand, touching the fingers tentatively, then taking them, curling his own small, brown hand over them when she didn't resist. "I reckon they stood up here on moonlight nights and drank beauty till they were filled with it."

She turned to regard his pinched, sharp face. "You're educated, ain't you?"

125

"Enough," he said, "to know a few things, but I got it from life and not from schools or books." He leaned back against the tree trunk, holding her hand, looking steadily into her face. "I saw a lot these past ten years."

"In the war?"

"In the war. Even before that, a little."

"Why do you stay with us?"

He quirked the little droll smile and shrugged his shoulders. "Why do you?"

"My paw's here."

"That's not a reason, Judith Anne. You've out-grown a need for him. You're a woman, not a kid."

She grew troubled and lowered her eyes to the ground. "I don't know . . . Maybe because of my sister.." She looked up swiftly. "Anyway, we daren't leave here."

"Aw, hell, Judith Anne, that's all over. I been chased by enough posses in my time to know how they work. Couple of days of riding all over, then they get disgusted and go home. If that's all you're worrying about, forget it."

"But why don't you go, if you know it's safe to?"

"*Quien sabe?* I like it here. It's restful. You're here. To see you I'd wait around the gates of hell for a blue-moon, Judith Anne."

She smiled and a flash of white teeth, small and strong and even, showed. "Don't you get

126

sick and tired of just sittin' around? I sure do."

"Naw. If I went away, where'd I go? The 'Nation? Back on the road again? It's quiet and restful here . . . " He pulled her hand a little so that she had to straighten her arm. He looked up the length of it to her face and tugged gently, a little harder. She went up against him until he used both arms to touch her, draw her still closer, but he was in no hurry—he had time—worlds of it—so he didn't hurry.

Down below and far out, a haziness hung over the land. Closer, he could see Matthew working without his shirt, sweat glistening off his torso. He was cleaning the creek and damming it up for a sumpage spot. The Kid smiled softly, watching the huge hulk of Matthew twist and turn with the grubbing of his chore.

Beneath the overhead where the Kid fondled Judith Anne, Old Man Fenwick and John Parkinson sat panting from the closeness inside the cool gloominess of the cave.

"There's a thing or two got to be done," the Old Man said.

Parkinson looked up briefly, heavy-lidded with sprawling listlessness.

"We got to get your girl and my boy back."

"How? Where are they? We don't know

127

nothing about them, Jacob. Maybe they slipped away."

"You know better. We all know better'n that."

"I don't." Parkinson grunted and closed his eyes.

"Well, I do!" the Old Man boomed and there was a rushing in his blood, a wild craftiness in his sunken eyes. "They got them in the settlement. Bunsen's got them!"

"Maybe. What can we do about that?"

"Go down an' get them out—that's what."

Parkinson opened his eyes, rolled his head to look at the Old Man and saw the throbbing vein in his temple, the working of his mouth—damp and slitted. He blinked and worked his way upright.

"They'll be thicker'n hair on a dog's back down there, Jacob."

"But we'll be wiser, John. We'll be like wraiths in the night. No settlement man ever come close to matching us and ours in stealth—you know that."

Parkinson scratched under his ribs and peered inside his ragged shirt at the great cords of flesh. When he looked up again the Old Man was on his feet, towering. There was a white flame of light in his eyes.

"I'm going to tell Matthew."

He hurried off, down the twisting, well-worn path and John Parkinson's rheumy eyes clung to his back until the mattrix of creepers, reaching, clinging, rich with thorns, swallowed up everything but his bobbing head beneath the shapeless old hat. Then Parkinson lay back and closed his eyes again and when his throat filled he coughed and spat sideways into the accumulated char of their many cooking fires.

"Matthew! Matthew . . . "

"I'm here. What is it?"

"No, leave the musket be; it's not an alarm."

Matthew came out of his crouch slowly, looking wide-eyed at the Old Man. "Well, hell . . . " he said, half in disgust, half in relief, "I thought it was trouble."

"We're going after Carl."

The son's eyes puckered and probed the Old Man's wrinkled, weathered countenance. "Going after Carl . . . Where?"

"Osage. Bunsen's got him there, boy, in his hog-pen of a jailhouse."

"How do you know that?"

"Don't question me—I *Know!*"

Matthew drew up erect, plunged fists into his pockets and there was something in his face that had never been there before. "Wait a little," he said severely. "You brought us to this, paw; let's let it all die down. Then we can round up our stock and push south into Texas and commence over again."

The Old Man stood stock-still, staring.

"We lost maw and Carl and Ellie. We lost a lot more, too, but that ain't important. Let's not lose everything, paw."

"Everything? What kind of talk is this? Would you rather live on your knees than die on your feet—answer me, Matthew—would you?"

"If I got to answer—yes. I'd rather live like a dog than die a fugitive."

"Matthew!"

The exploding fury of the Old Man's stare was deadly. Matthew cowed under it, but only by looking away from the wild face of his father. His words droned on.

"You don't know Carl's down there. You got an idea he might be. And there's something else in the back of your head, too. I got no way of knowing what it is, but I know it's there. You want us to go down for other reasons, too, not just for Carl. What are they?"

But the Old Man would not speak. For a long moment he stood there erect and stony, then he whirled and went hurrying up the path.

Matthew stood in thought a long time before resuming his chore of erecting a little dam across the creek. But the stones slid through his fingers and roiled mud obscured his vision and sweat stung his eyes so that he finally flung away from the spot and began trudging upwards towards the cave.

From the corner of his eye he saw movement and threw out a darting look in time to catch a short glimpse of Judith Anne descending the crooked trail from the overhead. He stopped briefly, gazed past her up the hillside, then quirked his mouth down hard and bleak and went on up to the cave.

John Parkinson saw him loom up in the opening, shirtless, burnt leather-brown, swelling with power and mightiness, and pushed past with his saddle balanced across his hip. Matthew flung out an arm, caught him and swung him half around.

"Where are you going?"

"To saddle up," the 'breed said. "We're ridin' for the settlement."

John went on out and Judith Anne stepped inside, halted to look sharply at Matthew. "Where's your shirt? What's wrong?"

"The Old Man's leading us to the settlement," he said coldly, "and it don't make sense."

Seeing rebellion in his face she smiled antagonistically upwards. "Don't it? Scairt, Matthew? Ellie's down there—and Carl."

He whirled on her with fury thick in his

131

voice. "How do you know that? How does *he* know it? And if they are, what difference does it make? They're safer there than here, aren't they?"

"Maybe. Maybe if Carl's hung, he's safer."

"Hung! You fool. If he's still there at all he's in their jailhouse. The Old Man said that!"

"Then we'll get him out—him and Ellie both."

"Judith Anne, listen to me. If we go down there and stir them up, they might hang somebody. Leave them be, dammit. And suppose we do get them? The country'll be up again. We can't always get clear . . ."

"Trouble in here?"

It was Marcy, small and languid-moving. Behind him the Old Man stomped to a halt, face craggy and stubbled with a salt-and-pepper beard. It was the Old Man who spoke into the silence. His words rang with scorn.

"He's been down there by the creek thinking. I raised a boy to *think*!" He pushed past Marcy and shouldered Matthew out of the way. Back in the duskiness of their cave the Old Man's saddle lay. He was making for it when Matthew lunged out and caught his arm, white with anger.

"Matthew, damn you—leave be!"

"Paw—don't! You're making it worse."

"Take your hand off me!"

132

"When you quit this craziness, I will."

The Old Man's free arm swung swiftly. Twice the boney fingers cracked against Matthew's face and the Old Man wrenched free. "You damned whelp! You ungrateful . . . !"

With a fearful roar that drowned the Old Man out, Matthew lunged forward. The Old Man stepped back, thunderstruck, but not for long. His scraggly fist swirled up and out, jolted squarely into Matthew's jaw. It only shook him. It didn't stop him nor even make him waver. Then the Old Man side-stepped like a cat, face livid, drew back his fist and fired it a second time. Matthew saw it coming and went under it with his big arms out, fingers crooked. There was a flung-back trickle of blood along one cheek from the corner of his mouth.

No one spoke; no one scarcely breathed. Kid Marcy drew Judith Anne back, pale eyes alight with strange pleasure in a thirsting, irrational way.

But the Old Man's blood was roaring in his head as it had roared a hundred times through fifty years of fighting. He was long in the tooth at this game and sidled out of harm's way while throwing looping, battering blows that Matthew made no attempt to duck. Finally he drove his father back, back, deeper into the cave, absorbing punishment, boring in.

133

Then the Old Man tripped in his own bridle-reins, flung down carelessly across his saddle, and Matthew's grunting breath hissed out as he bent. The Old Man scrambled frantically, but groping fingers found him, closed like iron around his legs and drew him forward through the pall of scuffed-up dust.

The Old Man twisted and scrabbled and wrenched this way and that. He knew what was coming for it was the way men fought in the land. Matthew lifted him almost bodily, strained to hold the wildly wrenching form, turned aside his head and pushed it hard against the Old Man's rags to save his eyes from clawing fingers. Locking his arms around the Old Man, he slowly, inevitably, began the squeeze. He crushed until muscles leapt and quivered snake-like while the Old Man's breath whistled out and a rain of futile blows landed upon Matthew's head.

Matthew crushed inward until his father's eyes bulged, his mouth fell open, all pink and wet with snags of discoloured teeth showing. The lips became blue below mottling cheeks.

A great gasp from the cave opening went unnoticed by father or son, but Marcy flung around, arms out spider-like, as John Parkinson halted wide-legged, unbelieving. Then he swept past the Kid and Judith Anne, swung

134

his pistol overhand from behind Matthew. The crunching sound was all that they heard; the short-arcing blow all they saw, before Matthew collapsed and his father fell free, writhing ponderously, almost inertly, but still conscious.

Marcy's expression remained a mingling of pleasure and wildness as he looked at the big sprawled bodies. Judith Anne's eyes showed horror when her father moved out of the way, for the Old Man was struggling to sit up, but Matthew's face, lying sideways, was purpling with colour and the angling streak of blood on it was drying dark.

"Why didn't you stop it?" Parkinson asked the Kid.

For answer he got a shrug, a crooked smile. "It wasn't my affair."

Parkinson gazed at the Old Man. "Give me a cup of water," he said to Judith Anne.

Marcy watched the 'breed pour most of it down the Old Man's chest. "Are we riding?" he asked.

Parkinson answered him without looking up. "To Osage."

"Me too, paw?" It was Judith.

Her father swore when he answered. "For Christ's sake, you can't stay here, can you? Go on, get saddled."

When the Old Man could suck in air he

135

looked over where Matthew lay. There was a soft moaning, a whimpering, coming from the battered mouth. "I'll kill him, John. God's my witness, I'll kill him."

"What started it?"

"He don't want to rescue his own brother; his own flesh and blood."

"Then leave him here."

"I figure to," the Old Man said, leaning heavily on his only friend. "Help me up . . . The whelp . . . To his own father, John. His own father."

The cave spun lazily and flecks appeared in the air. The Old Man blinked wetly, owlishly, and let out a long rattling breath.

Matthew rolled over, opened his eyes. They were pooled-dark with pain. He put a hand awkwardly to the back of his head and regarded both older men in silence until he'd explored the gash in his scalp.

"You, John?"

"Yes, me."

"Can I have a drink?"

John filled the tin cup, held it out. There was no pity or remorse or even any particular awareness in his face until the Old Man spoke, in a distant, rumbling way.

"We're leaving, Matthew. This is the road you chose—ride it! Ride it alone. A man who wouldn't even try to help his own flesh and blood . . . Let's go, John. Help me with my saddle."

Kid Marcy appeared for a last time in the entrance to the cave. He looked sardonically at Matthew, who was buttoning his ragged shirt, avoiding sunlight because it pained his eyes.

" 'You comin', Matt?"

"Who sent you?"

"No one."

"What do you care whether I come or not?"

"It's pretty simple. Five guns are better'n four guns."

With self-loathing, Matthew started for the daylight. The Kid watched him weave drunkenly, then went back, got Matthew's saddle and followed after the larger man.

When he joined them they were all mounted, as deathly still in sound and motion as night. Marcy was the only one who looked at him, who talked to him, and for Marcy it was ironically amusing that the two had fought. No such a thing as loyalty lived in him anywhere, so it was just a fight. There was nothing in his remembering blood at all, except half-shadows of destruction and killings, all tones of grey—no kind of filial feeling or loyalty.

Matthew rode listlessly and his face felt raw, his head ached with a great haze of throbbingness in cadence with the deep, strong pulsing in his heart.

They wound down out of the bracken with the dying day keeping them company. By the time they came to clear country, Marcy and Matthew were at the trail. Ahead of them rode John Parkinson, ahead of him Judith Anne, and foremost, shirt-tail out, cloth rent and dirty, head swinging like the wary head of a spinner-wolf, the Old Man.

Full night descended before they rode in ghostly file past the gutted stone house, squat and evil-ugly in the glow of a pale new moon. The Old Man stared granite-like as they passed. There was a whispering voice within him, an echo filled with desolation. He squeezed his eyes closed and bobbed along in time with the moving of his mount.

Back beside Matthew, Kid Marcy said, "After this, I'm leaving." When Matthew didn't respond, he added: "I never met a person like the Old Man before."

"I hope you never meet another."

"He's like an old fox."

"An old wolf."

"Why'd you fight him, Matt: you couldn't stop him—didn't you know that?"

"I knew it, I guess. I just didn't think about it." Matthew gazed at the ground, watched it sliding past. "He's always been right. Ever

138

since I can remember, the Old Man's always been right."

"Now you don't think he is?"

"It's more'n that," Matthew said softly. "He's changed. Been changing lately. Since we fought them at the house; maybe even before, I don't know."

"You lost faith in him?"

"That might be part of it, Kid. I don't want to talk about it."

"I do. I got no hankering to bust into Osage and find an army waiting for us."

"That ain't it," Matthew said. "The Old Man's better'n Indians at things like this. I got the feeling I been on the wrong side of the fence with him most of the time. Like he was wrong in things he did and I wasn't grown up enough to see it—until today. This riding after Carl: what will come of it even if we rescue him?"

"And the 'breed girl."

"It'll get everyone up in arms against us again. "Worse'n that . . . "

"Go on."

"I know my paw, Marcy. It ain't just for Carl we're going down there for. He don't have that kind of feeling for anything. I know that now. He just plain don't. There's something else in his head."

"What—do you think?"

139

Matthew wagged his head. "I don't know. I just know how his brain works. He's got some crazy notion—secret-like. He's always been like that, but lately it looks to me like he's been getting stranger."

"Crazy, you mean?" the Kid asked, face turned, eyes bright and sparrow-like.

"I don't want to talk about it."

The Old Man led them Indian-file through the silent night. He told them nothing, hadn't spoken to any of them since they'd ridden away from the hide-out. Out ahead like he was, none could see the tears that blurred his vision, the bitter working of his mouth from which no audible words fell. Even the night aided him, for it hid the fact that he was shaken, which surely would have been noticed in daylight.

When a sprinkling of golden light showed far ahead, winking, writhing down the miles, the Old Man swung northward and no one questioned his lead. They all followed, still in single-file, although the plain was broad, free of brush, and with only a rare scattering of trees. Followed in silence but more alert now, more steeled and hushed.

Only Matthew looked puzzled when the Old Man kept to his northerly course, even after they were nigh the settlement. Marcy should have been perplexed, for they both knew the jailhouse was southward, towards the tail-end of Osage, not northerly, where the shacks were scattered far apart, but Marcy was hypnotised by what the skinny, sharp moon outlined of Judith Anne, riding up ahead. He was heeding nothing else and his lips were wet with memory.

Matthew thought of spurring forward, correcting his father's course, but in the end he shrank back, followed along. Even if the Old Man didn't scorn him with the sunken eyes, he'd have an answer. You couldn't speak against him for he had a way of saying things with a burning zeal, and soon you doubted if you'd ever been right. Or his towering silences . . . And right now that was what deterred Matthew the most. The long look, the bleak silence.

Then the Old Man began an angling course down towards the farthest shacks. Matthew's puzzlement increased. His forehead was crumpled with lines, his brows down and straight across. Then Kid Marcy sighed and lounged back in his saddle and gazed out and around them. He straightened slowly and darted glances out an back and finally spoke aside in a hushed tone to Matthew.

"What the hell's he doing up here?"

"I don't know."

"Well, Christ, Matt, dangerous enough to

come here at all, but to waste time riding plumb around the place . . . "

"Be still, Marcy. Just watch him."

The Old Man was leading them right among the widely separated shacks, picking his way with his head low and swinging as though he'd lost something and was seeking it.

He'd go close enough to a shack to cast stones upon its roof and peer down in a hard way, then he'd draw off and rein towards the next one. Finally he stopped, sat still by the little hovel with its askew stovepipe and clasped his hands upon the saddlehorn.

Behind him Judith Anne halted, twisted and looked back at John Parkinson with a dark scowl. The 'breed looked from Jacob's back to the house and shrugged. When Marcy and Matthew drew in around the others the Old Man turned, watched them stop and ignored Matthew as though he was dead.

"I'm going in here," he said quickly. "You watch front and back. If a man runs out shoot him."

Matthew leaned forward in the saddle. "Why? Who lives here?"

"No matter to you," the Old Man said with dull fire.

"Bunsen?"

"Not Bunsen." The Old Man swung down,

flung his reins to Judith Anne and gestured for the others to obey him.

Marcy rode slowly around the shack, more curious then troubled. John Parkinson kneed up beside Judith Anne and watched the Old Man cross through the trampled weeds to the front panel of the house, lift a fist and roll knuckles over the door.

"I think I know who lives here," he said to Judith Anne, in a near-whisper. "A widow woman; little shrivelled up thing, only about half there in the head."

"Well, what's the old man want in there— lie with her, Paw?"

"You're talking dirty lately, Judith Anne."

The girl didn't hear. She was watching the door open. A spatter of lamp-glow struck the Old Man and bounced off him. There was a big shadow moving up behind him. She saw that, recognised it. "Matthew," she said swiftly.

"Be still."

The Old Man spoke softly to the little woman who was frozen in awe before his glare. There was an urgent ringing to his voice. "Send him out here, ma'am."

"Who? Who do you want? Who are you?"

"I didn't come here to stand and talk," the Old Man said with leashed harshness, keeping his voice down with a struggle.

143

"Send him out here!"

She began to shake and he brushed past her. Matthew followed, still wondering. Inside, there was one rude room. A rumpled bed along one wall took up most of the space. A blackened iron cook stove across the way faced a rude table. Tin cups hung from bent nails. There was a stale, greasy odour to the place. The Old Man looked giant-like in the middle of the room. He had a black pistol nearly a foot long in his fist and murder in his face.

The little woman backed into the room, away from the clotted shapes on horses out in the night. Her hands were pressed palms-flat against the smooth-board wall.

The Old Man ignored her. His glittering eyes were fastened to an ajar door where normally the commode set was. The big pistol lifted, swung to bear and he called out:

"Come out of there, you murderer!"

Matthew edged closer. One hand rested upon his holstered pistol. There was a quaking behind the door. He sensed it.

"Come out before I drive you out! Be quick now!"

The little woman began to sob and the door swung wider. Harry Cumberland stepped out barefoot in ragged underclothes soiled from long wear. He looked down in a fuddled way

144

at the weapon. His face was puffy from sleep, and red looking. There was no fear in his expression; just disbelief and astonishment.

Marcy came cat-footing through the rear door, gun out and cocked. In front, John Parkinson stood, filling the opening with his massive torso, head thrust forward as though listening.

Matthew's eyes lost their cloudiness. In a soft, strangled way he said, "Paw, you can't!"

The Old Man was unheeding. There was a fullness to his face, a voluptuousness of cruelty.

"Set them against us, didn't you, Preacher? Led them out to attack us . . ."

"Don't hurt him," the Widow Harris moaned. "Don't hurt Preacher Harry." The huge men, with their black guns, looked terrible to her in the wickering light. She moved back and forth along the wall, rocking herself and hiding her face behind small, dimpled hands.

"Preacher Harry," the Old Man intoned heavily. "If you know a prayer that'll let a stinking man's soul into Heaven, by God, you better say it now."

The Widow Harris whined in a quavering monotone: "No, no, no, no . . ."

"Don't, Paw. For Christ's sake, what are

145

you doing? We came here for . . . "

"I'm doing *this*, damn your meddling, Matthew. I'm doing *this!*" The gun tilted back still more and Preacher Harry was white to the eyes. Where his underdrawers hung around thin legs, he quaked finally, for with the coming of total understanding his spirit crumbled completely.

"Fenwick . . . In God's name, listen . . . "

"To what? Excuses? You low-down scum, Cumberland. You dirty scum . . . What are you doing in this woman's bed? What kind of a god you got that allows such as this, you filthy whelp. You with a wife and family!"

"That's what I'm trying to say, Fenwick. Listen, I can't die. I got others . . . "

"They'll be better off with you dead, you trash. Here in this woman's bed." The Old Man's voice was straining against the urge to boom out, to roar and thunder and crash. There was spittle like white suds at the edges of his mouth.

It was hopeless, Matthew knew. Every sign was upon the Old Man. Nothing short of a bullet would stop him. He turned away with a corroding heart. This, then, was what the Old Man had kept locked away in his secret mind. This murder . . . Not Carl, but this plain, preconceived murder of a man his father had come to fix all their troubles upon. Harry Cumberland.

" . . . No, no, no, no . . . 'God's right, not man's . . . No. No. You can't do this. You can't . . . "

"You got five seconds to make that prayer, Preacher," the Old Man said finally, his chest labouring, eyes white with a fierceness not rational at all. "Five seconds, you scum!"

From the door, John Parkinson said, "Where've you got the Old Man's son and my youngest girl?"

Cumberland seized upon it in the agony of desperation. "I'll take you to them. I'll get them out for you. I'll get them both out for you . . . "

"In the jailhouse?"

Cumberland began to nod so hard his beard jutted and danced in the orange light and the Old Man fired—just once.

Matthew heard the keening scream of the widow before John Parkinson slapped her, hard, and she buckled inwards, not from the blow, but from unconsciousness.

It stayed in his mind when he stumbled out to his horse and leaned across the saddle. There was no immediate recollection of the shot. Even the picture of Cumberland going down in a heap without a sound, didn't come back right away. It was the scream of Widow

147

Harris that stayed.

Kid Marcy rode around the building to the side of Matthew's mount. "Get up," he said excitedly. "Maybe someone heard that damned shot. A knife'd been better. Come on, Matt—the others are going."

Old Man Fenwick was the last to leave. He stood in the faint moonlight reloading his pistol and listening, throwing up his shaggy head to peer far out where other shacks were. He had doused the lamp and the house was as dark, as still as a tomb. Inside his head there was a sensation of relief; of brooding done with. *They can hate me*, he said to himself. *They can hound me—which they will—but Harry Cumberland won't ever scare another woman away from her man with his posses and his big talk. He won't ever drive another settlement to seek the blood of men like me—and like mine. Never . . .*

He was almost cheerful when he grunted up into the saddle, took the reins from pale-faced Judith Anne, missed her look of horror completely and wheeled his horse after a hard glance to see the others were coming.

John Parkinson reined up to ride stirrup. "To the jailhouse, Jacob?"

"To Bunsen's," the Old Man said. "Do any of you know which house is his?"

Matthew flung forward with black wrath in

148

his face. "That was murder. You can't do it again."

"But I will," the Old Man said. "I want Bunsen, too. If you had hot blood you'd want him even more."

"Good Lord a'mighty, paw . . . !"

"John," the Old Man roared above Matthew. "Where's he live?"

"I got no idea." Parkinson said, seeing life stirring in the town as they rode closer. "Listen! Let's get Ellie and Carl out. There'll be time for Bunsen later."

"You fool. If we don't do it now—tonight— we'll never get the chance. They'll be out after us like a pack of hounds come dawn."

Kid Marcy spoke up from beside Matthew. "Fenwick, Parkinson's right. If we take too long, we won't get 'em saved at all. I don't care, it isn't that, except we came here for a job. Going after Bunsen'll ruin the rest of it." Marcy flagged with one arm. "Look down there. They must've heard the shot."

Matthew saw the shadows of people hurrying helter-skelter through Osage, but he wasn't thinking of the danger when he spoke to Marcy.

"He don't care about saving lives—he wants to take them."

Marcy fell silent for a moment, then he made his crooked little smile and shrugged.

149

"It don't matter," he said.

Judith Anne stopped her horse. "It's already too late. Look."

The settlement was quickening with movement. Men called out as though a soughing wind had come to whisper to them of what portended. The Old Man watched, riding steadily towards them, but still far enough away so that he was only a horseman to them, not Fugitive Fenwick—yet.

In his mind words ran together to form a dark beauty from violence, twisted and smoking so that he couldn't tell whether they fell from his lips or were phantoms. Hurried words made from the warp of his secret mind, his hidden soul.

"Cumberland drove her off. Bunsen took my youngest. Settlement men have hated and feared me for years. I have been plundered by Secesh and Yanks. I have fought to survive and I *have* survived and I *will* survive. It is in me to survive. I had no hope for music, for pleasure. I come early to know it wasn't for me or for mine. I raised men out of boys . . . Not Matthew; not Matthew after all. Carl I never knew well . . . There was in him a softness. Matthew . . . "

"Jacob! Listen to me, Jacob! Something's roused 'em up. If we go much closer they'll know us."

"Shut up, John, I'm thinking."

Judith Anne flung her horse between the Old Man and her father. She wasn't the sensuous 'breed girl now, with the power to fire men, for her face was ghastly and her flying hair like cables, like snakes caught up by the heads and writhing.

"Paw' we got to get away. Some of 'em are a-horseback. They're riding this way. Come on, Paw!"

Parkinson's face glowered at the riders seen dimly far ahead. He turned, finally, ignoring the girl and seeking the Old Man's face on her far side. But he didn't speak and the Old Man kept right on advancing, detachment making his expression blank and mild appearing.

It was Matthew who jogged up, leaned and yanked back on the reins so abruptly the Old Man was flung forward in the saddle. His eyes snapped around and grew hot upon Matthew's face.

"Are you scairt to die like a man, damn you?" he demanded.

"There's no call to die," Matthew said sharply. "You undid what little good we might have done. Now come on. Look there—at least twenty of them and all riding up this way."

The Old Man turned his head to stare at the horsemen trotting solidly through the night towards them. His face cleared suddenly, became stark and iron-like again. "To the west," he said brusquely. "Ride west and follow me."

They went clattering over the summer-hard ground with a sound like far-off thunder and got lost in huge reaches of prairie westerly from the settlement. The Old Man didn't draw up until the others protested that their animals were staggering. From one extreme he seemed to have gone to the other; to want to flee to the ends of the Territory.

They found a marshy creek-bottom and Kid Marcy went afoot among the tree-growth until he found what he sought. A single pistol shot brought down three plump grouse from a covey. He plucked them in the pale light of a tiny fire Judith Anne had built, used a tin pot from his saddlebags to stew them in and kept stirring the fragrant mess with a willow bough. Matthew lay flat on his back upon a swear sweat-limp saddleblanket. He spoke to no one. John Parkinson watched Marcy stir the stew with a hypnotised stare. Judith Anne kept her face averted and the Old Man remained standing, listening, head cocked in the familiar stance they knew well, then quite suddenly he left them walking southerly through the tanglement of trees, willows and creepers. None of them looked up to watch him go.

152

"Get the cups," Marcy said to Judith Anne. She moved to obey and her father crowded in closer to the fire. They ate together, the three of them. The Old Man didn't return and Matthew spurned the offer of food when the Kid held out a steaming cup to him.

Afterwards, the edge gone from hunger, Parkinson went out to look at the horses. Judith Anne helped the Kid mop out the cups with switches of dry grass.

"He's strange all right," Marcy said, speaking of what was uppermost in all their minds.

"Not strange—crazy. Didn't you see his face back there when we were going towards the settlement? He was sort of smiling. He'd have led us right in among them. He's crazy."

Marcy peered into the cup, saw its shiny bottom and laid it aside. "I reckon everyone's a little crazy, Judith Anne."

"No . . . Not crazy like he is. He'd have got us shot, sure."

"It don't matter," the Kid said, arising. "Come on. Take a walk along the creek with me."

She looked upwards swiftly. "Maybe you're crazy, too," she said tartly, but without conviction. "Half the Territory hunting us down the night and that old man out there brooding somewhere, and you want to take a walk along the creek."

The Kid smiled at her. "It's better'n sitting here waiting for the sky to fall on us, ain't it? Come on."

She got up, moved around the fire and went with him. She was a head taller than he, but only half as graceful. Matthew rolled up on his side and stared at the dying fire, the rank smell of horse-sweat in his nostrils.

CHAPTER SIX

When the Old Man came back, light-footed, all tall and dark with shadows around him, John Parkinson was still by the dead fire.

"They still hunt us," the Old Man said.

"You saw them?"

The Old Man dropped down with a headshake. "I didn't see them. I went back down a few miles and put my ear to the ground. They're riding, John, they're riding."

Parkinson humped over still more and behind the Old Man where Matthew lay, there grew a stirring.

"Paw, what ailed you back there? You were riding right into them?"

The Old Man didn't explode; didn't even turn around to face his eldest when he answered, for inside his head, the voice was

154

speaking and he harkened to it. There's a wealth of weariness in you, Jacob. You've led them, shielded them and now you're tired. *She* left you. Your youngest is gone and the harlot who robbed him of a soul—she's gone too. And this other one hates you . . . The others, too, in time.

A darkness bowed him down and he rode his spirit.

"I do what is best, Matthew," he said in a terribly mild way.

The words rang heavy as stone in Matthew's heart. He lay back again and didn't stir until faint rustlings in the underbrush up-creek roused them all. Parkinson went flat behind his rifle and the Old Man arose, stood majestically upright with the black pistol bared. Matthew rolled over, knowing, but with his gun out nonetheless and when Judith Anne stepped into the clearing he let the hammer fall back with its little snippet of sound, gazing past her.

When Marcy came into the moist light from a sickly moon, he stopped and squinted from face to face. The Old Man looked like doom. His lips moved, his slag-like jaws worked without sound and from up around his seamed eyes, there was a cold bright arcing.

"You are godless," he said, and sank down without looking at any of them again.

Parkinson stared beadily from behind the rifle and said nothing. The small wetness of his mind strained with thoughts until he shook himself and got to his knees, brushed leaves from his front and hunkered closer to the cooling char.

Matthew was too dulled to feel anger or indignation. He watched the sinners go back out a ways and sit down, whispering together.

When the Old Man thought the horses sufficiently rested, he ordered them all to saddle up. It was an hour before dawn and none had rested. Their legs dragged, their fingers were clumsy with cinchas, with bits and headstalls. They all moved to do his bidding without questioning and he led them slowly over the unfamiliar ground hugging close to the screening of trees and jungle along the creek until the sky paled. Then he made for a little knob and stopped atop it.

An uneasy wind strode up and down the land before the sun came, and then it dwindled, but refused to die. Matthew sniffed it from habit and thought Fall was coming. A new droplet of life enlivened his spirit for a moment, because of all the seasons, he loved Fall the best. It had the unrestrained wildness of colour, the tang of wind and dawn-chill, the savour of Indian fires in secret glens, the smokiness of many camps where savages

156

worked fast at jerking meat against Cold Face to follow.

"Look there," the Old Man said.

Matthew was tugged back to reality with a start. There had been bleakness to the words.

Little bands of horsemen, scattered and bunched up, not more than ten to a band, were criss-crossing the land. Like soldiers, Matthew thought. There's a brain behind the way they're doing that.

He watched several clutches ride across the creek at intervals and out the far sides and onward. No tree was left unscruntinised.

Marcy spoke reminiscently. "It's like old times," he said, watching, clear-eyed and calculating. "Only they don't wear blue." He looked at Matthew with a haunting smile. "Skirmish order."

"Bunsen was a soldier," the Old Man said. "I've heard that said many times."

Matthew nodded. It would be the sheriff. In his mind's eyes, he recollected the savageness in Bunsen's face, the uncompromising ferocity. "We'd better keep moving then," he said. "Westerly."

Parkinson cleared his throat and gazed at the Old Man where he sat like iron in front of them—still and erect and watching the little motes moving far off.

"We'll move," he said thinly. "We'll do it

157

like we did before. They hunted us day and might and the earth swallowed us up. It will again."

"How?" Matthew asked. "This is unfamiliar country, Paw."

"*This* is . . ."

"You mean go back to the cave?"

The Old Man was silent a while. "No, not that far back, Matthew. They'll be between us and the cave now. Not that far back . . . We came down here to do a job!"

Matthew drew up, unbelieving. Before he could speak, the Old Man jumped his horse out. They went streaming down the dawn like avengers, the Old Man far out in the lead and behind him, John Parkinson, with his daughter flying at his side.

Kid Marcy rocketed along beside Matthew and when the eldest son swore in a strangling way, Marcy looked across at him. "Like a fox," he called out. "Your old man's crazy like a fox, Matt."

"You fool . . ."

"Uh, huh, he's right. You don't know about these things. Look, they got men all over the land, scouring it for us. They stripped their settlement bare to feed a gibbet." Marcy laughed.

"But we got no friends in Osage, Marcy. Every hand down here's against us."

"Means nothing," the Kid retorted. "I got a lot of faith in the Old Man. He's a fox, Matt."

The Old Man led them craftily back and forth in a way that kept them hidden while they angled southerly. Not until the sun was burning high did he take his final course — northeast towards Osage. By then they were under his spell again. Even Judith Anne, who loathed the Old Man—and he her—rode without questioning, while John Parkinson exulted, for it was always right with him when responsibility lay in another's hands.

The Old Man drew up in a tangle of whispering trees where the little wind worked high overhead and his strange eyes were brittle-bright. "There," he said quickly, "see them behind us. Down here the land's been scarched."

"I can see the settlement," Parkinson said, very straight and straining in his saddle, rifle teetering across the fork.

Matthew squinted to make out buildings. They were low in the distance, huddled together in immensity as though fearful. It's just possible, he thought. Marcy might be right; the Old Man might carry it off. God, it would be good to see Carl again . . . And Ellie? His gaze clouded. Why had he allowed Judith Anne to persuade him to betray Carl to her sister? Conscience dug him hard. "Let's get on," he said. Then to his father: "After we get them—what?"

"I make no plans ahead," the Old Man said. "Life is how you find it."

He led them with the guile of Indiandom; with the still watchfulness of cold deadliness planning each step. When they came to the last thicket before the brushed-over land behind the southern-most shacks, he made them get down and check their arms. It was a wasted moment, for even Judith Anne had been holding her pistol in a damp palm for an hour, while the sun climbed steadily towards the meridian.

They found a stinking sumpage where green scum and bones of animals lay, and while the smell was overpowering, there was a rank growth there to hide in. They squatted behind the Old Man.

Close ahead were people puttering around their shacks. A fat slattern came to a door and cast out slops from a tin washbowl. A man scratched in the flinty soil where anemic vegetables grew. They could even see lingering puffs of smoke from his pipe in the dazzling clear air.

"Quiet now," the Old Man said. "Don't shoot. Don't make a sound. The jailhouse's up a ways. We'll work along this patch of brush until we're close behind it."

They had to crawl in places, for the brush was sparse, dust covered and dying. Among its clinging shoots were broken pieces of pottery white as bones, but sharper, and debris of many kinds. Kid Marcy snagged his ragged shirt and tore it more, which made him curse. Sweat dripped off their faces. Matthew kept worrying about retreat, for they'd left the horses tied back in the trees. Afoot, he felt naked. If there was serious trouble, escape back across the vacant land would be impossible. Half the village would be shooting at them. He flung sweat off his chin with a jerk of his head.

"We're getting close."

Then the brush ended and a scalded strip of dusty earth lay between them and the buildings on either side of the jailhouse, limned sharply against the pale sky. They lay flat with pounding hearts. Kid Marcy wiggled up to his knees and touched the Old Man's arm.

"There's a rider coming."

The man loped slowly towards Osage from the direction of the manhunt. They watched him swing wide into the settlement, go clattering down the roadway and halt near a saloon where other men hastened up and clustered around him. They all went inside.

John Parkinson smacked his lips and the Old Man scowled at him. Kid Marcy sat back

161

more comfortably. "Maybe others'll be giving up, too," he said.

The Old Man ignored the voice and near him, Matthew kept a hard vigil until, shortly afterwards, the men came out of the saloon and called to one another, hurrying different ways, while the rider mounted, spun his horse and walked it slowly back the way he'd come. Into this the Old Man read meaning for he nodded his head up and down.

"He came back to tell them something. They've found where we camped last night, I expect."

When the body of horsemen loped vigorously westward from Osage, the Old Man's eyes grew slitted watching them.

"Now," he said. "Now!"

Matthew got up and walked flatly out of the brush. There was clinging dust on him. When he slapped his clothing it squirted outwards in transparent clouds. He trudged behind the Old Man and all of them were watchful. The last out of the sage clump was Kid Marcy. He caught Judith Anne's hand and pulled her back.

"Stay here."

She looked doubting, for such was her revived belief in the Old Man—despite her fear and hatred—that Marcy's words were empty to her.

"Stay here in case someone's got to fetch us the horses. If there's any shooting, bring 'em up fast. Don't stop for anything, but bring 'em up."

He hurried past her after the others and Judith Anne stood there with her pistol dangling, perplexed and hesitant. Then they were too far away and she drew back deeper into the covert, watching.

The Old Man stopped near a steel-strapped door at the rear of the jailhouse, looked back at Marcy and Matthew and John Parkinson. A quick frown drew down over his gaunt face.

"Where's the girl?"

"Back by the horses. She'll bring them up fast if anything goes wrong."

"You told her to do that?"

"Yes."

"Goddamn you, Marcy," the Old Man stormed. "I'm captain here. I told you that!"

Matthew pushed forth. "Go on," he said urgently. "Hurry up!"

But the Old Man stood a moment longer with black fury in his face before he swung closer to the steel reinforced door. He dropped his head to listen before he raised the pistol barrel and rapped sharply. An echo came back hollowly with silence in its wake and the back of the mud building was airless

163

and blazing hot where they stood breathing shallowly.

"Who's there?"

"Bunsen," the Old Man said in a short and muffled way, "open up."

There was a sliding, a creaking, and the panel moved a little. The Old Man flung his shoulder forward and Matthew heard the grunt and gasp that came next. Kid Marcy whipped past him with a whiteness in his face where the crooked smile showed ghastly. His pistol was up and cocked.

Inside, it was cool and dark with a smell of dinginess. With the exception of John Parkinson, they all recognised the jailer with fat rolls hanging greasily along his chops. He panicked, blue eyes were wide and dry, in a staring way; his mouth twisted still from the impact of the door against his paunch.

"Don't yell out," the Old Man ordered. "John, take his gun."

Out of nowhere a knife glittered, sank swiftly and in the stunned silence, they could hear it ripping flesh, grating over bone. Matthew half turned, disbelieving. Then the jailer fell in a heap and writhed. His eyes bulged, but he made no sound, although his mouth was open and the cords straining in his neck.

"Marcy!"

164

The Kid sprang away, a tawny wolf of a man, wispy and made with excitement.

The Old Man stared downwards, watched the trickle of scarlet a second, then locked his face against it and turned away. "Go look, Matthew," he said. "John, stay by that door. Call me if anything looks wrong." His eyes searched the gloom for Marcy.

Matthew sucked in gulps of air, but the iron band of internal coldness wouldn't be relieved. A burning flared in his head. He didn't hear the startled voice until half past the gloom cell.

"God alive—Matthew! *Matthew!*"

"Ellie . . ."

She was straining against the steel, the fullness of her mashed taut.

"What are you doing . . . ?"

"Where's Carl?"

"In the other cell."

He whirled away from her in time to hear Kid Marcy speaking low and tensely.

"Here he is, Matt. Get the key off'n that jailer."

But Matthew went down where light shown through the high slot of a window and looked at his brother. Marcy glanced swiftly upwards then scurried away.

"Carl!"

"Matt! Listen, Matt, you got to leave here."

165

Carl's face was dank with sweat, pale and twisted.

Matthew turned. "Hurry up, Marcy," he hissed.

"It ain't on him," the Kid said swiftly. He straightened up as the Old Man came up. "The key ain't . . . "

"Go look in that little room by the roadway then," the Old Man said with a curt gesture. He stepped past the dead man and stalked down the little corridor. Ellie caught his eye with movement. He glared around and sharp annoyance crossed his face like a shadow. He didn't speak.

Matthew moved back as his father approached and Carl gripped the bars with white knuckles. "Paw, *get out of here!*"

"We will," the Old Man said, and jerked his head at Matthew. "Go find that damned key—hurry!"

"Listen, Paw . . . !"

"No time for talk, Carl."

"You got to listen!"

Matthew was going past Ellie's cell when she reached through the bars straining, clutched at his shirt and caught the cloth. "Matthew! It's a trap. Please . . . "

He wrenched away and took two strides before he drew up and stared back at her.

"It's a trap. Listen to me. Sheriff Bunsen's

166

got men across the road. We heard his planning this last night, Matthew. He said you'd try to get us out . . . "

"Paw!"

"Lower your voice, Matthew."

"Damn it, Paw, come here a minute."

The Old Man moved swiftly towards Matthew, his face was tight with care. The colour was leached out of it.

"She says it's a trap."

"I know. Carl just told me."

"Kid Marcy burst out of the office with a large bronze key in one fist. His flushed face was alight. "Here."

The Old Man snatched at the key, whirled away from Matthew and his incoherent mutterings were audible as he went up to Carl's cage, reached for the heavy lock.

"*Jacob!*"

Over his shoulder, fumbling with the lock still, the Old Man said, "Matthew, go see what's wrong with John."

Matthew glimpsed the Kid's expression of wonderment as he flung past him. He heard Ellie call sharply to Marcy.

John Parkinson was crouched, the rear door opened a slit.

He beckoned from behind with his hand. "Look out there, Jacob."

"It's Matthew."

167

"Look out there!"

Matthew looked and his breath whooshed out. A tightness in his chest was hurting. "Get the old man," he hissed. "Move, damn it!"

When Jacob came he brushed Matthew out of the way, knelt all stiff and forbidding looking, the black pistol in his fist. For a moment he was motionless, then he said, "They got her. Seven of them and they found your girl out there, John." He got up heavily and glared over their heads. "How, I wonder?"

Kid Marcy came towards them in a springing way. Matthew looked down into his face and read a foreboding there. "Are they onto us?" Marcy asked. Matthew nodded.

"They got Judith Anne. That means they got our horses, too."

"Oh, hell," the Kid said and it sounded ludicrous. "Ellie says they're across the road, too." He peered at the Old Man. "Now what?"

"How did they do it?"

Matthew's anger was riding high. "How? Why, dammit," he said, "there's only one way they could do it. They back-tracked us, Paw."

John Parkinson stood stiffly erect, hand on his pistol. "We got to get out of here. They got the rifles, too, if they got the horses."

"Rifles be damned," Marcy snapped. "Come on."

"Wait!" the Old Man commanded and Marcy stopped in mid-turn. "The next time you give an order, I'm going to kill you!"

"There's no time for this," Matthew said, laying a hand upon the Old Man's sleeve.

But the wrath was slow dying in the Old Man's face. Finally, he turned towards the opened door that led to the roadside office. "We'll look," he said. "if there's a way out it'll be across the road—among the buildings on the other side."

Matthew followed the long striding form. "Ellie said . . ."

"I know what she said, but the road's narrower than running back out the way we came, you fool. And if we got back to the brush—there are no horses. We got to have horses!"

They strung out in the office. A great hush had descended. Kid Marcy broke it finally, with terrible oaths. "Bunsen, I knew he'd been a soldier. Christ, how easy he done this. It makes me want to . . ."

"Shut up!"

Matthew stared blankly at an empty rifle-rack. The wall was paler where guns had been. That, more than all the frightening sense of being trapped, brought home to him how it had been worked out beforehand. He groaned and moved towards a barred-window

169

where John Parkinson was crouched peering out.

But there was nothing to see—just sunshine as brilliant as spun glass. The plank walks were empty. Storefronts shimmered without movement. The settlement lay still and waiting without a sound anywhere. Sweat trickled down between his shoulders. The butt of his drawn gun was slippery with it.

The Old Man moved like a caged cat, springy in the knees, head high and canted, eyes moving with liquid flame in their depths. His jaw bulged from the tightness of locked teeth.

Matthew straightened up. "Paw, they'll send word to the others they got Judith Anne—that we're in their trap."

"I know, I know."

"Then *do* something!"

"Hush, boy."

The Old Man touched Kid Marcy with his fingers. "You're smallest. You'll make the least target. Listen to me. We got to have horses. Got to. You go out that door and zig-zag for cover. Get us something to ride."

"Hell," the Kid said, standing erect with his odd, crooked smile, "a man wouldn't get ten feet from here and you know it." The pale eyes were fearless, pale-bright. "You never did like me, oldtimer. Well, I got no fear of dying, but this is crazy—me rushing out there."

"We can't stay here, Marcy," the Old Man thundered, backing up like a cornered giant. "They won't even have to gun us out of here. This is a trap. They'll starve us out. When we're hungry and out of bullets—they'll cut us down like dogs when we march out. Are you blind, man? We're all dead anyway!"

The spell of words streaked with fury and desperation rang into Marcy's skull, rattled there where it was dark and hot. His grin hung up at the edges of his mouth when he nodded. "All right, I'll go. A bullet's better'n a hangrope."

"There's no time to lose."

Marcy turned towards Matthew and John Parkinson. "Cover me," he said. "If I had some money I'd lay a bet on how far I'll get."

Matthew's throat was raw and dry. He knew—they all knew. There wasn't a chance in the world for Kid Marcy to make it. Not a chance.

"Fenwick, where's the other boy and John's girl? Let them out. Two more guns might help. I'll need all the cover I can get."

The Old Man's stare was feverish. "That key don't work," he said.

Marcy chuckled. "Bunsen thought all this

171

up? Even to the fake key?" He started across the room, put a hand on the bar of the door and faced them. "Listen, I've known a long time the rope was payed out. I been hanging by the knot for a long time. It don't matter a hell of a lot. Not really. I never thought it did matter. A man comes here, cuts his swath, goes out. All right, I've cut mine . . . Cover me, boys."

He shot the bar, drew the door back and threw himself past it with a curdling rebel yell bursting from his throat that shattered the unearthly stillness. Through its shrieking quiver the Old Man stormed at the others.

"Give him cover! Shoot at their flashes and pray to God! Take aim to end life—not to live too long yourselves."

Matthew was crouched by a window with his gun-snout resting on the sill. The Old Man's words dinned into his brain. He knew without looking around that one of those slavering spells was upon his father. He could pinch close his eyes and see the spray of spittle, the twisted face crumpled with lust and insanity and a strange intentness, like the Old Man was listening to something Matthew nor any other, could hear.

"Aim low and mind—no snap shooting. Use your rear sight, boys," the Old Man thundered.

172

Matthew forced himself to look out where unkind light from a pale sky shone; where Kid Marcy was running. It stung him suddenly that there was no firing. For the space of a withheld breath he didn't think there would be any, then a wispy puff of smoke spewed, and another, and another—with flat, powerful sounds behind them. More shots until the daylight was sifted of them and they fell without rhythm, slamming-hard and lethal.

"*Now!*" The Old Man was screaming. "Give it to them—*now!* Take mine from me will you, Harry Cumberland—Bunsen! I'll teach you there's more'n flesh to a body. I'll teach you . . . 'teach you . . . !'"

Matthew fired twice at a spigot of flame across the way. After his second shot there was a convulsion, a rattling and writhing, then a stillness. The din of gunshots deafened him. It was like before, in the stone house with the black-powder stench choking them, burning-hot and gagging. The difference now was that Matthew no longer had hope or faith. Three against an army . . .

The Old Man's groan was loud.

"He's down. Oh Lord—he's down!"

Matthew saw the wispy form wilt. In his heart he winced as slugs tore into Marcy's flesh, twisting him, holding him suspended until more slugs came to lash into the numb-

173

ing body. Then he was down. Flat-down and unmoving with dust spurting around him, lazy and yellow.

But it was the Old Man's groan that seared him for never before in his life had he heard his father give over to despair. Never once . . .

"John! Matthew!"

Parkinson got up ponderously and let off a strange and frightening sound. There wasn't a man on the frontier who didn't know the meaning of that sound. The gobble of a turkey-cock made by an Indian was warning of impending doom.

But the Old Man's voice, high and resonant, drowned it out. "Come over here. Move fast now."

They crowded up by him. The Old Man's face was splotched with veins and dust and caked sweat. "We got to go out. There's nothing left." He laid a corded hand upon the door-bar, crooked the fingers there like talons. "Now listen to me," he said, with dry-tears running down his face, "make for the livery barn and get to horse. Don't stop if one of us falls. Get astride and ride for it. Don't stop for nothing. Ride west as far as a horse'll take you then keep running afoot. Stay together as long as you can. We got strength so long as we're together."

Matthew's head had Widow Harris' keening scream ringing in it again. He wasn't conscious of moving when the Old Man threw the bar up with a crash and plunged out into the turmoil of smoke and thunder. Didn't hear men burst into hoarse and exultant screams as the three outlaws fled northward along the plankwalk firing at puffs of smoke, at flashes of fire.

He was aware of nothing until a familiar pungency filled his head, its ammonia overtones clearing out the fumes and numbness and worse. The Old Man was plunging deep into a barn up ahead. Behind him loped ungainly John Parkinson. A blurred, unfamiliar face appeared and dissolved in a burst of flame from the Old Man's hand.

"Horses! Yonder in the tie-stalls," the Old Man cried out, making for the dingy coolness where quivering animals strained at tie-ropes. Matthew saw him yank off the rope, twist up a squaw-bridle furiously, fling himself aboard bareback and whirl the beast.

John Parkinson was cursing when Matthew fought a horse who plunged and snorted. He let go the terrified animal and raced for another one as John swept past, arm rising and falling.

Matthew's fingers felt twice their normal size and without joints. He tried frantically to make a squaw-bridle, but the rope fell into a series of knots so he twisted up a simple loop, yanked it down upon the horse's nose and struggled to get his seat, spun the beast with a slap across the cheek with his hat. The horse let off a crackling snort, flung its head and went careening out of the back of the barn, a hundred yards behind Parkinson and the Old Man.

The excited settlement men who were firing at his father and the 'breed were startled when a belated third rider burst out of the turmoil close to them, hand-gun spurting and thundering. In the seconds it took them to recover, Matthew goaded the horse into gigantic leaps that flung back clods. Then the guns boomed again, bullets sang past, spearing onward through the hot, roiled air.

Matthew was gaining when the Old Man cried out and slammed his lathered beast back upon its haunches. Coming towards them in a blurred race was a great host of riders. The dark sweat upon their horses was visible even beyond gunrange. It was the men Bunsen had led out to search for the renegades. Matthew leaned far over and his horse shot past the Old Man, going northerly, for the westward route of escape was cut off now. Parkinson came up next, and last was the Old Man, an ungainly figure, squared into the rushing air, arms flopping and head thrust forward as though to

176

aid his flight by sheer will alone.

The pursuit held level for an hour then began to drop away. Cries of rage and frustration rose softly in the lengthening day. Matthew's gun was empty and he had not bothered to reload it. His attention was directed to the horse he rode. Peering over his shoulder and watching the distance widening, dead hope revived. It hadn't seemed possible they would all emerge alive. It hadn't seen possible that *any* of them would, back in Bunsen's jailhouse. Now even rifle balls couldn't reach them and each leap of their animals widened the gulf. It was miraculous.

He laid low along the horse's neck and squinted his eyes against the sting of whipping mane. Fashioned a war-bridle, thumbed it into place and straightened up. Eased back upon it until he felt the beast responding, then he looked around.

The Old Man's shirt-tail was whipping behind him. His long, thin legs were around the animal under him like coil springs and his shaggy mane of hair flew like a speckled grey banner.

Off to one side, John Parkinson rode low on his horse, bent far over. He had both fists wound into the beast's mane and clenched there tightly, next to the rippling hide.

The Old Man slowed, swung his head and

177

squinted backwards. "The Lord was with us," he said in fierce triumph. "Head for those uplands, Matthew. I think John's been hit."

They made it into a bosque of wind-whipped cottonwoods. Matthew tied his horse back from view, caught the lead-rope to the Old Man's animal and made it fast also, then strode down where his father knelt. There was a soft duskiness to the sky and a little fat star hung low above the thickening shadows.

"He's hard hit, Matthew."

Oh Lord! Matthew stood transfixed staring down at the gaping wound, uncovered and jelly-like where the Old Man had peeled back the soggy shirt. Oh Lord!

He knelt across from the Old Man. For a moment he was gripped with an illness, then he bent and attempted to staunch the gush of claret, wiping it with wide strokes only to have it bubble upwards and roll across the great-corded belly again and down the quivering flesh.

"Clean through him," the Old Man said with awe. "From behind."

"Be quiet," Matthew said. Then: "Go find some water." And when the Old Man had gone off he looked into the 'breed's face, saw the blue tint to his lips, the pinched-down closedness of his murky eyes, and thought screaming things in his own mind that were deafening in their silence.

You're dying, Parkinson. The Old Man's gone to fetch you water, but it won't help; there's no use to pant like that. We'll be here with you—we'll bear the vigil after your spirit's gone down into the grass. That's two today, you and the little wisp of a man who believed in nothing. There'll be more, Parkinson. You've lost two daughters; was it in you to realise—to care? I think not; I think you're like the Old Man—only without his will, his craftiness, his courage. Oh, you had courage, Parkinson—Indian courage; all red, frothy, without feeling; the kind that would slap a half-crazy little widow-woman and turn aside. The kind to peer down into Cumberland's contorted face and feel nothing but an odd satisfaction that a Will had been done. That kind of courage.

And Judith Anne's like you, in ways. She's a splinter off your spirit with callousness blind-deep in her warp. Nothing'd change either of you but this . . .

You're brought low for no particular reason, Parkinson. You lie here for no cause, no pull of the blood; only because you were like all of us, wound around by the Old Man's will. Blinded by his spell, caught up and flung here

179

like an autumn leaf because he held you in the bondage of his—

"Matthew?"

"It's me. Lie still. The Old Man's gone for water."

"I don't see you well . . . They got us?"

"No, we're clear. We're safe. Lie quiet now."

"I'm afire."

Afire? Is that what it's like, Parkinson. It didn't smash your spine so it went through your soft parts with nothing to stop it. I got no idea what's inside you, Parkinson, but I can feel it, all sloshing red and drowning.

Parkinson began a faint, quavering chant. A toneless thing that rose and fell and trailed off and each time Matthew thought it was stilled, then it would come back again, eerie, an ageless humming that went down deep into a listener, found response in forgotten, dark places, drew out a thin, dim memory of primitive things eons distant. Then it stopped and the night grew soft with a soughing wind dragging through the cotton-woods and Parkinson rolled his head from side to side, eyes clamped tight.

"Water. . . ."

"It's coming," Matthew said. "The Old Man's fetching it."

"Christ! What happened?"

"You're shot. Quit tossing, John, lie quiet."

"We got away."

"Yes, we got away."

"Judith Anne—got away?"

"They took her, John. She'll be safe in their jailhouse." *Safer'n we are, Parkinson. You're dying man; she's the least of your worries.*

"How bad am I shot, Matthew?"

"Plumb through. Back to front."

"I'll die."

Parkinson began the chant again and Matthew looked downward wondering what slow, primitive thoughts swirled in his mind in this sundown hour.

The Old Man returned noiselessly, stood above the dying man a second, heard the dull humming and dropped down. Matthew took the hat full of water, lifted Parkinson's face and poured some across his mouth. The chant choked off, Parkinson's eyes flicked wide open and he began to gulp, to choke and swallow with prodigous effort. Swallowed after the hat was emptied and its last brown dregs gone; until Matthew laid him back. There was a roaring in his head the others couldn't hear. A dimming to his mind. He started to chant again. It swindled softly on a high key, faded away and John Parkinson lay dead.

Matthew went low to search for heartbeat and when there was none, he straightened up, rocked back on his heels and watched the swarthy face relax, grow soft and mellow with a beauty, a peacefulness if had never possessed in life. And the body flattened, widened. A finger of night-wind ruffled Parkinson's black hair and moved on.

"He's dead."

"Yes," the Old Man said, "and it could be me, for the peacefulness it brings."

Matthew turned away. "Harry Cumberland saw nothing peaceful to dying," he said.

From his crouched position, the Old Man glared upwards. "No man has any grace to him, who dies in sin!"

"Now you're God," Matthew said, looking straight out where darkness lay, his back to the Old Man and bitterness in him like poison. "Now you're going to say how men should die."

The Old Man came up off the ground. Breath whistled past his nostrils. "Between you and me, there's been little enough lately," he said. "Don't defile the air where John lies, with your hatred."

"I've got no hatred. It's defeat I got in me, not hatred."

"You're the first of our blood to have it, I'll covent you that."

"Maw didn't?"

The Old Man's great bony fists knotted. "It

182

was Cumberland and those with him scairt her off and you know it."

"I don't believe that," Matthew said, facing around. "I don't believe it and I don't think you do. She'd been too many years in Oklahoma—in that stone house. It wasn't fear made her leave. It was despair. It was defeat. Fighting every waking hour against something she couldn't hope to win out over."

"What? I ask you what couldn't be won out over? We come here with nothing but our bare hands."

"You. She couldn't win out over you, and neither can I."

Matthew went into the trees where the horses were. He took them one in each hand by the ropes and led them out where cured grass shone tan and thick under a swelling moon. While they grazed he hunkered between them and through the long vigil only one sound interrupted his thoughts. The Old Man was dropping stones over John Parkinson's body. It went on and on for hours, at longer intervals as the Old Man had to scour farther out to find them. The dull thud of stones upon stones—until the cairn was finished. Then he pictured the gaunt frame kneeling, arranging rocks, fitting them, forcing them into place.

How many dead now? Three that he was

certain of at the stone house. Three and maybe another three; others he didn't know about. Harry Cumberland, ragged underwear flapping around spindly, blue-veined legs. That made four And in the settlement fight he knew of one himself, which made five. And John Parkinson. Six dead. Seven, counting Will Parson, but you couldn't count him, for none of them had done that. Six then; dead for what?

Because of a madness in the Old Man's head, which had grown stranger these past days, weeks, months. His answer to everything—an upraised fist, a snarled word, a roar of defiance.

Matthew squatted low in apathy and listened to the still, tiny voice, of memory. Felt hunger that wasn't only for food. Knew that some place along the back-trail he'd lost something out of himself. Something which had always been strong and bright and confident; something with bright, golden courage to it.

Youth.

He'd lost youth, that's what it was. Somewhere very recently, youth had dropped away from him. It was harder to smile, to laugh. It was more difficult to see beauty, to see high colour and dancing light and no longer would his outstretched arm encounter warmth and faith in all he touched. Youth was gone and it would never return.

Maybe it'd fallen away in the cottage of Widow Harris; maybe up at the cave. Maybe even before that—at the stone house when he'd heard that his mother was gone — or after Carl was no more.

One of the horses threw up its head and a cold finger brushed gently over the man's heart. He froze motionless, the gauze dissolving from his mind. There was something out in the night. Then the second animal raised its head, little ears flickering nervously, pointing forward, northwest, rigid while the animal's nose sucked at the air, drew meaning from it.

"Matthew!"

It was the Old Man hissing close by, but invisible.

"Matthew, bring those horses back into the trees and be quick."

He obeyed, staying between the beasts, moving stealthily with tiny pimples bursting out over his body, touching cloth and magnifying its coarseness so that a burst of some strange current emanated outward into the darkness from him seeking contact with another aura—which was peril.

"Here, give me that rope."

The Old Man was holding out a spidery arm towards him.

185

"What is it?"

"Something; I don't know. I was back in the trees sitting—looking out where you were. I seen the horses get troubled. He forged a rope-bridle as he spoke, big hands moving with sureness. "It might only be wolves or coyotes."

"And it might be men. We been here a long time."

"Yes. We'll ride west along this ridge. Keep to the trees until we're beyond whatever scairt the animals." The Old Man turned and looked straight at Matthew. "Two left out of seven, but it lies at the hands of no man to beat a Fenwick."

Matthew's horse threw up its head. A mighty arm shot out, caught the animal's nostrils, closed down cruelly and for the space of several heartbeats the two men stared whitely into each other's eyes. Then the animal began to fidget and Matthew slacked off.

"It's men, or horses with men on them," he said. "The horse would have whinnered in another second."

"It'll be riders. We left plenty in their settlement to stir them into riding the night. Come on, Matthew."

"For now we'd best stand fast. They'll be waiting for movement." He saw the Old Man draw up, stiffen. "I know," he said quickly, in

186

a strong whisper. "You're captain here. I got no right to make an order."

The coldness drew down across the Old Man's face. "Don't mock me, boy," he said. "I've got years behind me you lack. I do what's best."

Anger seared Matthew so sharply that he shook. The hand over the horse's nostrils quaked in a tightening spasm. The beast flagged with its head, but the fingers were slow giving over. The face slower to drain of black colour.

"Listen, Paw, you've done what's best since we left the cave. There're two now, where seven stood. If that's best, then it'll get me and you killed, too."

"*Matthew!*"

"I used to take your part against Carl. God forgive me for that. It was Carl was right, not you. I wish I could do it all over again; by God, I'd humble you proper. I'd break you to lead, damned if I wouldn't!"

The Old Man raised an arm. For seconds his big fist hung suspended. There was a snarl of fierceness to his face.

"Don't Paw! If you hit me again, I'll break your neck. So help me, God, I'll break your neck with my hands. I mean it. I mean every damned word of it. You didn't lead us—you destroyed us."

187

The Old Man lowered his arm. Stood stiff and unbending for only a second, then he whirled, lashed down with the rope-bridle and sprang upon the stolen horse, turned it and went cat-footing out of sight among the giant cottonwoods.

CHAPTER SEVEN

Matthew stood there listening until the faintest sounds were no more, then moved in closer to the horse for companionship. It was the first time since he could remember, that he was completely alone. His mind, despite the danger, went back down the years with a poignancy he couldn't fathom. Days faded into nights, then grew light again, time growing into years, spinning out lazily, heavy and solid with memory. Times he and Carl had gone poke-berry gathering for their mother. Days making lye-soap, stirring oak ashes into the cauldron. Of speaking little but knowing each other well, he and his brother. A richness of familiarity growing between them with mutual silence, and until this moment the Old Man's shadow had always been there.

Other faces shadow-like, faded and glowed, but always somewhere nearby in the background, between him and trouble, the Old Man, oaken and gnarled and sunken-eyed; all fierce and mighty-like.

Then the spectre yesterdays dissolved and there was just the stolen horse beside him and silence fading into deep darkness with a faint, sighing wind out a ways.

He stroked the matted mane, smelt horse sweat and night. Where there had been seven, one now stood, and somewhere behind him a swell of rocks shone dully beneath a lustreless moon, where Parkinson lay. Somewhere else, down the dark twisting of trees, the Old Man was gliding westerly to freedom and escape. Easterly, down the lift of land he'd come over last, were Carl and Ellie—and Judith Anne.

There came a quick clatter of metal and he stood up straight, as startled as a hawk. Whatever was out there was approaching the bosque. Remembering how the settlement men had criss-crossed the plain made him tingle. He had to move, not westerly as the Old Man had gone for the sound had come from that direction, but easterly, so as to keep ahead of whoever was out there looking for him. Cautiously easterly, as silent as a ghost, for now there was only the weak darkness to aid him.

Alone beside the horse, he shivered a little and dread touched his spirit with a coldness.

189

He led the horse softly past Parkinson's cairn, past the running dip of land they'd raced up a few short hours before, and melted into shadows.

Walked ahead of the horse until he thought it safe to mount, then clambered upon the beast's back and pushed it gently over the spongy ground with matted shadows to screen him, and hope revived.

But only briefly, for suddenly there came a great crashing back in the trees, a wild turmoil of sound and his heart turned black with fear. He leaned forward and the horse shot out belly-down, little ears flattened. Rode with the night hurtling past, a big knot of dread in his throat because shouts rose clear and sharp behind him.

Later, when the sounds died away, he was loping across open country where there were occasional houses. Once a great slavering hound paced him with lolling tongue, baying in a booming way until Matthew reined southerly and lost the dog with a burst of speed. Again, where several log houses were cluttered close by one another, he went furtively afoot, leading the horse for extra silence. Clear once more, he thudded over the rolling prairie with the moon over his right shoulder as a guide.

The world had never seemed so foreign to

him as it did that night. The stars lacked warmth. They were too high, too far off and smidgin-small, for kinship. The moon was wan and curled in a sickled way, sightless and dour. Only the horse beneath him was friendly.

When he began a great quartering of the country east of the settlement, meant to bring him back to familiar country and perhaps eventually to the cave, his weariness grew solid and burdensome, for as the Old Man had said, *they'd* be swarming over the land now.

He stopped several times, put his ear to the earth and held his breath. The last time he heard the beating of a solitary rider coming towards him from the west. He strained to hear more but there was only that one short sounding.

A lone rider might mean anything or nothing. It might even mean the Old Man had met up with their pursuers, been turned back and was fleeing like Matthew was, heading for familiar country. It might be just a traveller; perhaps a messenger taking word of the grave among the cottonwoods; someone heading for the settlement.

For a time, Matthew sat like stone, then restlessness plagued him for each lost second was precious. The trouble was he no longer knew which way to go. Finally, he rode deep into the closest brush patch, angled up a hump-backed ridge and squatted there, looking out and around.

Below and to his right was the dust smeared road to osage. He thought it likely the lone horseman was upon it somewhere, although he caught no sound, or sight of movement. He rode carefully down through the sage a quarter of a mile to the edge of the road. It was pale and empty as far as he could see in either direction and that increased his worry so he got down and listened again. There was nothing but deep silence.

While the darkness could be his ally, it could just as easily be his betrayer. If the rider he'd heard had been a scout or a messenger going ahead to rouse the countryside in front of him, at any dip or rise in the prairie, Matthew might come face to face with a posse. It did not occur to him that each mental obstacle he was erecting sprang directly from the helplessness deep within him, which in turn sprang from the sense of loss and futility occasioned by the Old Man's departure.

He sat there like an Indian, with his single rope-rein hanging loose, with his body aching from stress and his belly as flap-empty as a wet sack, nerves raw, brain magnifying each small sound so that when huddling birds in the sage made scolding music, it sounded as loud and ominous as the report of a rifle.

Then a slow-growing clatter of horsemen came whisper-soft from north up the road and he spun the horse, forced it blindly deeper into the brush, dismounted and stood erect with one hand on the beast's nose, and his heart was thudding. The sound grew stronger, went echoing down the road towards Osage long before he saw them, a dark, rhythmically pounding host.

Soldiers!

They came rumbling forward in a long line of twos with a little bird-tailed pennant in their midst and sweat-faded uniforms made ink-black by the night. They approached with a swinging sound no other body of horsemen made, metal scabbards clanking, accoutrements, rubbing in harsh sibilance, a purposeful cadence peculiarly their own. Matthew's heart sank.

There would be no escape. Not with the land swarming with settlement men, riders from outlying places, now soldiers as well. One man or a hundred men couldn't get clear. He grew light-headed with the certainty and the desolation of this knowledge. And if he fled these soldiers, got clear of them, escaped the other bands of manhunters, eluded ten posses, there was still no escape, for men would hunt him, hound him, so long as he remained free, for by now he and the Old Man had become notorious, a challenge to every manhunter in the Territory. In time, there would be rewards.

Only if he made his way to the Cherokee Nation would he find surcease. But he was no outlaw; not in his heart and mind. He had killed, yes; to survive. That was the law of the frontier and he'd come to manhood knowing it was right, but he was no outlaw, no renegade. The thought of mingling with men of the 'Nation was abhorrent, as it had been with the Old Man.

The soldiers careened past in a long, slovenly line. There were no words, no signs from any of them, just the rise and fall of men on big horses, whose faces were hidden in hat-shadow, whose white gloves looked like thick hands of bone. A winkling of swaying saber scabbards.

With a gasp he threw himself upon the horse, ground it cruelly with his heels, tearing out of the brush and down into the roadway, where dust curled upwards, hung briefly suspended, rank and thick. Reined up a hundred yards behind the last soldier and threw up his arm.

"Hey! Hey, soldiers—hold up!"

Went racing after them until he drew up on the near side and saw their startled faces swing towards him, their puddled eyes glistening deep in shadows.

"Hold up!"

A voice soared above the din of riding men, others took it up, tossed and husked it the length of the line and finally a flinty bass roared out far ahead, horses broke over into choppy gaits, slowed, halted.

"What is it, back there?"

"Settler, sir. Hollered for us to stop."

Matthew watched the sparse, thin man riding back down the column towards him. There was no kindness in the face at all. A monstrous up-curling moustache made it look brutal, inhuman.

"What do you want, settler?"

"I'm Matthew Fenwick; I want to give up."

The officer stopped, hooked a gloved hand in his belt and gazed stoically past his big moustache. "Is that so," he said. "Well; that's fine, because we want you. Hand over the gun."

Men's necks craned. A whimper of sound went along the line as Matthew held the pistol out, butt-first, and the officer took it, looked at it, hefted it in his gloved hand.

"Where's your old man, Fenwick?"

"I don't know. We parted."

"Why'd you part—or are you lying?"

"I'm not lying. We just parted is all."

"Where is he? Where'd he head for?"

"I don't know."

"Don't lie, you Secesh scum."

"I'm not lying, I told you. I wasn't a Secesh, either."

"You're all Secesh down here," the Officer said with a steely ring, each word cold and full of menace. "Damned rebel scum . . . Where's your old man?"

"I honest don't know, soldier. We parted a long ways back."

"And the half-breed—where's he?"

"Dead. My father buried him under a cairn in a bosque of cottonwoods where he parted. Parkinson was shot through."

"Good; one less." The officer's gaze dropped, went over the scruffy, tucked-up animal. "Stole that horse, too, didn't you?" He gave Matthew no chance to answer. "Sure you did. Stole that one and others. Fought clear of the Osage jailhouse and killed four men doing it. You're going to hang so damned high the crows'll build nests in your hair."

The acid tongue turned upon the soldiers nearest Matthew. "Corporal; five-man escort for the prisoner." Without another look at Matthew, the officer turned his horse, rode up towards the front of the column.

A big gloved paw closed briefly over Matthew's arm. "In here, Fenwick. Hell man—

196

you made us ride sixty miles on a handful of hardtack, with your cavorting down here . . . All right, that's good; now remember—you're a prisoner."

"I'll remember. I won't try to run off." Matthew gazed into the faces which were closest, powdered with dust and sagging with tiredness. "I surrendered, I won't try to run off."

The soldier grunted. He was red-faced and heavy in a square, shapeless way. There were chevrons on his upper arms. "You don't look like you or that horse could've stood much more running," he said.

"We're used up all right."

"Hungry too?"

"God-awful hungry," Matthew replied.

The red-headed sergeant groped behind his saddle with one hand. "I never seen a converted Secesh wasn't hungry. Why don't you people down here quit your infernal bickerin' and settle down to farming."

He handed Matthew several small, iron-like biscuits as a singing shout burst out and the column began moving forward. Matthew ate as he rode, towering above the weary-faced troopers on their big Army horses.

The column rode at alternating gaits for two hours, never stopping until they clattered loudly into Osage where late lamps burnt, showering the soldiers with pale orange light. Settlement men stood hushed and watchful as the column ground to a halt and orders rippled, dismounting the men. Plucking off his gauntlets the thin, tall officer walked down the line. His voice was like stone scratching across glass and there was antagonism in it; dislike thick enough to cut with a knife. Settlement men watched, listened, standing aloof without speaking, faces unfriendly and closed down with bitterness. many an ex-Confederate soldier looked down from the plankwalk. Memory was stark and vivid. The double line of Yankee blue did that.

"They got him! They got Fenwick!"

The shout was abrupt and loud. Other voices took it up, cast it in a thundering way back and forth across the roadway until the village rang with it. Men poured out onto the plankwalk, ran over into the roadway, began to converge upon the soldiers. A bull-bass demanded that someone ride after the posses and bring them back quickly.

The officer's face grew pale. "Get back, damn you," he shouted at the villagers. "Men; close up! Sergeant . . . *Sergeant!*"

"Yes, sir!"

"Sabres; flat of their sabres. No shooting . . . Get back you Secesh scum!"

A squat man as heavy as a boulder stopped

close to Matthew's guard. His legs were planted wide and he stared without speaking. Others bumped against him, careened off. Shouts swirled over his head, but he didn't open his mouth.

"There he is—in there. Drag the bastard out! Take him to the tree . . . Come on; they won't use them swords."

"Steady," the red-faced sergeant roared with a saber gripped hard in his mottled fist. "Steady boys; the flat of 'em now. No running-through . . . Here, you damned trash, back off or I'll lay your head open. Back off now . . . "

Matthew felt the closing up of the soldiers tight around him. Their quivers went through him, crouching there, unarmed, big fists balled and with a dry-sourness burning in his mouth. Words as big as trees grew stark in his mind. It was a mistake. He'd made a terrible mistake. This was crazy—they're going to storm the soldiers. They're lynch-crazy. 'Never should've done this.

"Hold!" The squat man growled loudly to those crowding up on all sides. His great voice trembled into the tumult. "Hold, I said! Leave off that shoving! Settle back a minute. They got him safe."

"They'll give him over or we'll take him," someone cried out, far back in the straining mob.

199

"They got him all right, and he'll get tried too," the squat man said loudly. "He'll get his—just wait and see."

"Tried hell! He'll hang, that's what he'll do, and we'll do it. No damned blue bellies—"

"Shut up that kind of talk. Listen a minute."

"Shut up yourself," a blond giant said, edging close to the squat man. "You and your talk."

From within the sabre-circle, Matthew watched the squat man face the towering blonde giant, cornsilk hair askew and tumbling. He thought they would fight. Knew the first show of violence would launch the lusting ring of settlement men upon the soldiers. Knew there was small hope for his life, beset as he was by the pack of human wolves.

" . . . 'Been seven of us killed by Fenwicks!"

"He'll be tried for it."

Shouts beat upon the angry night air, drowning out the argument. The tall officer edged closer behind the blond giant, his saber opened a way.

"You there! Get back and shut up. I mean that—*get back!*"

It wasn't the broadside of the saber which pressed taut against the giant's back as he faced around, sucking back from the sharp point and looking up its curved length of bright steel.

"Put it down, Yank. I'll thrash you till you beg."

The officer's face was white to the eyes, his mouth a flat slit, from which words squirted sharp and tense. "I'll do it, Secesh; I'll run you through. Now get back."

From behind, the squat man lifted an arm, caught at the giant's belt and pulled. "Don't force him, lad," the older man said. "Now then—that's better."

Matthew was bent low, ready to spring, to fight and batter and claw if the blue circle was breached. It was like a dream to him, the boiling sound, screams and howls, the glimmer of sabers softly curving and deadly bright. The panting, straining of men around him, their acrid smell.

Then it came—the breaching of their blue lines. Just when the soldiers close to Matthew began to catch a sweet glimpse of surcease. Began to hope the mob was coming round. Four horsemen thundered down the road, a vanguard of others returning to Osage, scattering those afoot like leaves and driving straight into the packed soldiers.

Men screamed and cursed and sabers went flying. Someone fired a pistol and in the next instant the crowd was locked in straining em-

201

brace and Matthew was struck from behind by a snatched-up saber, swung wrong-end to. The brass hilt and guard stunned him. He fought, staggering, against a whirling illness, a bursting roar within his skull. Knew somehow he must battle for his life and swung huge arms like flails, dimly feeling the crunch, the wet splatter from noses, mouths. Fought with his brain full of lights and crashing sound.

Blows that rained over him went un-felt and shortly there was a softness to tread upon and through the furious melee crept a moaning that grew steadily into a long mournful whimpering as the fight rocked this way and that, soldiers closing up over fallen comrades, sabers rising and falling, a few with liquid red tassels dripping from them.

While the soldiers couldn't rally upon weakened spots in their defensive circle—they were held nearly motionless by the crush of bodies—the settlement men could run around those motionless in straining fury and hurl themselves upon Matthew's guard. Soldiers went down swinging their sabers until they were lost underfoot in the writhing mass. Each time this occurred Matthew's protective circle grew smaller.

Then he was popped out into the battle like the seed from a grape. Stood shoulder to shoulder with his panting protectors and cut a ten foot swath in the attackers with his huge fists. His knuckles turned purple and dripped gore, but there was no feeling. Somewhere behind, a mighty shout went up. There was the crashing of many horsemen into the village from the prairie beyond. The earth shook with their coming and each hunter pealed a roar of triumph, eager, slavering for Matthew's blood. Their combined weight, along with the other settlement men, was overwhelming. Flesh and bone could not withstand the charge of their horses.

Matthew saw the red-headed sergeant's hat go flying and didn't hear the gunshot until seconds later—which seemed a lifetime. A roar bubbled past the sergeant's clenched teeth. He fought, wielding a big dragon pistol, his saber gone, and men fell before him like apples off a tree. Then he was sagging, doubling over and Matthew had more room to himself. He edged the injured man back, half protecting him, half fighting in crazed desperation to hold the shrinking circle intact.

His arms felt like lead, too heavy to raise, to aim, and there was a thin streamer of blood across one cheek. Suddenly a brawny man loomed up, mouth wide open, but without sound issuing from it. Matthew watched the wagon-spoke go up, up, up. He rolled away from it on the descent, heavily and clumsily, so that it crunched down the side of his head, ripped his ear and shattered upon his collarbone.

Hands were tearing at him, grappling like steel, rending his clothing, pushing, pummelling him forward, away from the remaining soldiers until he was gulped up by the crowd, shot farther away from aid and deeper into the writhing mass of panting, howling civilians. Without seeing it, he sensed they were bearing him towards the leaning cottonwood tree by the water-trough. He was right.

"We got 'im!"

He was butted through the horde and those who took time to look up, to see him, swung fists and cursed him wildly until he sagged from the blows and hung helpless upon the arms of those gripping him.

Out of nowhere the squat man appeared and planted himself before Matthew fending off blows until they were both under the tree, then he dropped his thick arms panting from exertion. There was now a maniacal look in his face to match other faces, but he still did not shout.

Those nearest Matthew drew up, sucking air in, and stared at one another. They left off shouting now and one of them said: "Get a rope."

"I'll get one. While I'm gone one of you fetch something for him to stand on."

The squat man was still standing there when two dozen hands strained to grasp Matthew's naked torso, white except for blood streaks, and towering mightily above them all. They hurled him up against the tree. A soft cascade of leaves fell. A man ran up with a snarl of rope, held it out uncertainly. The squat man took it without a word, began to fashion a coiled noose with strong fingers, nostrils flaring with each breath he sucked in.

"Ahhhh, Mark; you've changed your tune about him!"

The squat man's head shook negatively without coming up. "Not by a damned sight I ain't," he said, "but if you're going to hang him, then at least do it right. This knot'll break his spine. He won't dangle up there jerking and turning purple with his tongue out a foot."

Matthew held himself upright by clinging to the tree. He turned and looked at them, into their wild venomous faces and knew this was the end. Over their heads he saw the soldiers rallying upon their injured. There were sprawled bodies around them, trampled flat, mostly in drab settlement attire.

There had been no women in the crowd

before; now there were. They were huddling over bodies all racked with sobs and their wailing rose up his spine like steel fingers, over and above the husking of the feverish mob. Even above the groaning of the wounded themselves.

"Hurry up, Mark. Get on with it."

The squat man heeded not. His fingers, wise old spiders all hairy and blind, curled the rope until it stood created properly, a real hangman's noose. "All right," he said, flinging it down. "There you are."

"Toss it over the limb, somebody."

Matthew watched their eager haste, saw the cast fall short, heard their impatient mutterings and saw others try until the rope fell down the far side of the limb with a dozen hands seeking greedily to clutch its loose end.

The squat man looked up into his face without mercy, but without hate. He said, "Pray, big feller, you don't have much time."

Pray? To what? To the Old Man? What have I done wrong except fight to survive— which ain't wrong. What have I done . . . ?

"Give him a word," the squat man said as others bent high on tip-toe to cast the noose around his neck. The noise subsided somewhat for the vision of the mighty son of Old Man Fenwick brought to his end had a sobering effect upon many. There was still noise

206

aplenty, shouting and moaning and great, heavy sobs rending the pale sky with anguish.

He saw mingling hush and hate in their faces and opened his mouth, but there were no words, only great pain in his spirit and throughout his body. But his mouth hung agape, as though he'd say something. Those nearest thrust their faces close with morbid expectancy, eyes agleam, small and red with wolfishness.

"No, no, no . . . 'Not your right. No, no . . . It's warn't *him*, it was the Old Man. *This one* tried to stop it. Tried to stop the Old Man from doing it. This ain't the one—no—you got the wrong one."

She forced her little soft body in among them, pushing and pulling and working closer all the time with a macabre strangeness in her face.

"Listen to me; this ain't the one shot Preacher Harry, no, no. It was the Old Man. This one yelled for the Old Man not to do it. He wrestled with the devil against it . . . You can't hang *this* one; not him."

They craned around to see her, pitifully small and round, like a child who'd never grown up in the head, greying hair lank, soft eyes swimming in a strange mist, little dimpled hands clasped together in front of her.

The squat man reached out and drew her

up beside Matthew. "Now go ahead," he said to the mob. "You heard her. I tried to get you to *think;* now you heard. Go ahead, and when it's all over . . . "

There was a stir far back. Someone said in clear tones. "The soldiers; they're aimin' at us!"

For Matthew the crisis had passed. He looked out over their heads scarcely daring to hope. The soldiers had their muskets and those able to, were kneeling in a long row before others who stood behind them. The officer, with a dripping gash at the chin, was holding his saber high.

"Ready!"

Those far back broke and ran.

"Aim!"

The squat man came alive in a burst of movement. "Wait," he bellowed. "For God's sake, wait! Don't shoot! He's safe—your prisoner's safe."

The saber dropped a fraction, carbine butts snugged in closer, twin lines of blue men showed only a length of round steel growing outward from tight, white faces. There was murder in their eyes.

"*Don't fire!* There's your prisoner. There's Fenwick, over by the tree. He's safe. Osage surrenders. *Don't shoot!*"

Matthew watched the tall officer's face in

fascination. He felt detached from things around him, numbly apart, and the expression of naked wrath he saw gripped him. When the squat man got close it was as though he had to brace into that burning stare.

"It's done with, sir. It's all over. Take your man . . . It's all over with."

The officer spoke a one syllable word from the corner of his mouth and the soldiers relaxed. His arm came down slowly until the saber touched the trampled earth. He leaned upon the weapon, staring at the hushed, still people around him. He didn't speak to the shorter, broader man before him, but his eyes came back and lingered on that face.

"Sergeant!"

When there was no response he repeated it. A soldier in the line spoke up. "The sergeant's hurt, sir."

"All right. Corporal!"

A man limped forward, saluted. His hat was gone and his tunic was torn.

"Take Fenwick to their jailhouse. Lock him up, post a guard—a strong one—and pass the order. First armed civilian to approach the jailhouse is to be shot on sight. Shoot to kill, Corporal, tell them that, too. Do you understand—*to kill!*"

"Yes, sir!"

They led Matthew away, four soiled soldiers

with drawn faces and hating eyes. At the jail-house, a man stood beetling at them. One of the soldiers swung his musket-butt outward in a hard thrust and the man fell back.

Inside, the room was crowded with injured townsmen. Some looked up out of apathetic eyes, others in less pain, glared in thick silence. The musket-wielding soldiers ordered a jailer to lead them to a cell and when he hesitated, he swung the musket, smashed the jailer in the chest. He collapsed and the soldier lashed out with a booted toe that thudded into the jailer's ribs.

"Get up, you scum, before I kick you to death. *Get up!*"

It took two civilians to raise the jailer. His lips were locked tight in agony. He hobbled, bent over, to a nail in the wall, got several monstrous keys and led the soldier-party through the office doorway and into the gloom of the cell-block.

"*Matthew!*"

It was Ellie. He saw her dark-circled eyes and lagged back, but the soldiers gripping his arms, carried him along. Then their leader stopped with a wrinkled forehead.

"Only two cells in here?"

The jailer nodded without speaking. He was leaning upon the mud wall with colour pumping slowly back into his cheeks.

210

"Well," the soldier said, more to himself than to the others, "how do we pair 'em up? There's a girl in that there cell."

"What's the difference?" an enlisted man grumbled. "They're all scum together. Secesh scum."

A wiser head prevailed. "Put him in with her. Someone's got to do some patching on his hide and a girl'd be handy for that."

So they thrust Matthew into Ellie's cage and tromped back down the short corridor. Matthew heard one of them twist a key in the door-lock, closing out all light and most of the sound.

"What happened, Matthew?"

He told her, groping along the wall with his hand, seeking a pallet. His flesh was cut and gashed, slippery with blood and dry-hot to the touch. His bones ached and his head sang. There was a throbbing pain at the base of his skull where the saber-hilt had slammed up hard.

She knelt by him when at last he found the pallet, sank down upon it, lay back with closed eyes and listened to the bubbling of his own breath.

"Didn't they get your father, too?"

"No . . . We parted. I don't know where he went . . . What became of him . . . Ellie?"

"Lie still, Matthew. I've got a little water

211

here and some rags. Which wounds are the worst?"

"I don't know, Ellie."

She fell silent. Her hands were cool and gentle. They moved slowly over his torso, sopping up blood, wiping away filth, succouring him with cool water until he went all drowsy and limp.

He would have dropped into a slumber, but something kept nagging from deep in his mind. Something . . . Oh, yes; about her father. About John Parkinson up there under the cairn the Old Man had erected.

"Ellie?"

"I'm here. Rest quiet, Matthew; I'm trying not to hurt you."

"It ain't that. John's dead. Your paw's dead."

The gentle hands grew still upon his chest. Lay there without pressure.

"He got hard hit when we broke out of this jailhouse. Died in a clump of cottonwoods northwards a ways. The Old Man put a cairn over him."

Ellie eased back on her heels and twisted her head slightly. "Did you hear that, Judith Anne?" she asked.

Matthew opened his eyes and rolled his head to strain for sight in the darkness. "Is *she* in here, too?"

"She's here. Over in the corner."

He recognized the voice when the answer came back. "I heard."

That was all Judith Anne said and there was a coldness to the words, a sting of hatred. Matthew let his head roll back and stared upwards into the darkness and slowly closed his eyes.

Ellie bent low enough to make out his purpling face. She sponged it with a damp rag. "Carl was yelling. We could all hear the fight outside—men yelling your name. The jailer went down to Carl's cell. I think he beat him with a chain, because after he went down there, Carl was quiet."

"Call to him," Matthew said, struggling to rouse his mind.

"I did. He didn't answer. The jailer told me to shut up."

"We got to help him."

"Lie still," she said when he moved. "You're locked in here, so just lie quiet."

"It's hopeless. We're beat, Ellie. We're destroyed. The Old Man did that to us . . . I got to see Carl."

She pressed down upon his chest until the weak struggling subsided. "There ain't a chance, Matthew. Lie quiet and sleep; just lie quiet and sleep. You survived; Carl will too."

Survived? Yes, that was so; he'd survived.

It was a preachment of the Old Man's that they would survive. That it lay at the hands of no man to defeat Fenwicks. But that wasn't so. They were defeated, all of them; even the dead ones.

He exhaled a rattling breath and felt the cooling rag moving in a slow circle over his torn body. Slower and slower . . .

CHAPTER EIGHT

They hunted the Old Man in droves and armies, sought him in westering wagons by the light of the moon, with pitch-pine knots held high while they rummaged through the duffle of strangers, poked and peered anywhere a man might hide. They swept the country around the stone house, now rat-filled and sag-doored from looters. Even back out where hostiles were and some muttered the redskins were harbouring him. That he had gotten away to the 'Nation; was even now leading an army of renegades towards Osage to rescue his sons and drown the settlement in the blood of vengeance.

Captain Wilson of the Army, heard the stories that rumour spread and sent companies and squads to search also, even though he was sceptical, and for the soldiers there was no zeal to the chore. They despised Oklahomans nearly as much as Fenwicks. Felt each was a part of the other and all were scum. For proof they had a bulging jailhouse and a storeroom where the residue of those arrested for the riot were held under constant guard.

The land seethed and each breath of air brought new tales. The Old Man had murdered a settler and his wife in their bed, down-country a ways. He'd been seen upon a flinty ledge with the moon flowing behind him, grey and gaunt, an old wolf of a man holding high his gnarled fist, clutching a rifle. Again, he was raiding with hostiles, spreading desolation and terror across the far frontier, mane flying, fading into the night in front of a silent, fierce army of savages.

The summer days drew out like that and gradually it came to be accepted that the Old Man had escaped. There was a low growl about Matthew and Carl. They at least should be tried, executed. Captain Wilson had rein-forcements and he was brusque.

"When I'm ready I'll hold their trails," he'd told the settlement people. "Until then you stay away from the jailhouse or take the consequences."

But when Fall slipped in to chill things and the nights were a little longer, with the tang of woodsmoke fragrant upon the autumn air, he

215

began to hold hearings for those who had assaulted United States soldiers. Sentences were harsh, feeling bitter. People went to Pete Bunsen with complaints, but got little satisfaction for the sheriff was a bleak man and didn't hold with rioting, even against Yankee soldiers. So there came to be little groups of dissenters and Captain Wilson posted an order against foregathering. When it was defied, he struck swiftly and without mercy. More trails. Osage grew sulky, but by Fall, it was cowed.

And Pete Bunsen strode the roadway with frustration making his face more harsh than ever. It was bad enough to have soldiers in the settlement; it was worse that the fugitive he dreamt of, thought of constantly, had eluded every effort made to catch him. There was humiliation in that, for invariably, Bunsen had led the settlement posses.

He rode often, sometimes with posses, sometimes alone, except for the black hatred in his heart and oaths upon his lips for the Old Man remained a phantom, and while Bunsen knew he couldn't do half that was being laid to him, he also knew that so many divergent rumours were a better screen for the Old Man's whereabouts than any hideout he might use.

Moreover, there was the mouthing over his so-clever trap which had caught the quail and flushed them too, all in the same stroke. So cunning, with even a faked key to let out the 'breed girl and the other giant. All dismal, utter failures. Oh, but he'd had them under his thumb. He'd had them exactly as he'd planned it. Was it his fault they broke out, crashed through the livery barn on bare-backed mounts, riding like imps from Below? No; not Pete Bunsen's fault—it was the Old Man's fault—but settlement folks didn't say that.

So the sheriff had cause and reason to grow sullen and black with hidden fury. Behind his back, people spoke against him and it was the Old Man's doings, not his. People were doing the will of a grey old wolf and Bunsen rode long hours bending over tracks which the ground seemed to spawn, and finally he stayed to himself almost entirely and nursed hatred like it was something alive inside him.

Said little and encouraged those around him to say little. Racked his brain for a way to snare a big-maned old fox, while others also rode out, scouring the land.

"You're the one," Captain Wilson told him once, short days after the riot. "You're the one sent for help. It doesn't appear to me that you're doing much to find this old devil, Bunsen, sitting around the settlement on your behind and scowling at the dust."

It was senseless to argue. First, because Wilson was rawhide and sinew, with blue-bellied suspicion of Neutral Ground people who were mostly ex-Confederates, the mature ones anyway. And lastly, there was no point, or no wish, to say he'd ridden five times as far as any two of Wilson's troopers. So he'd said nothing, but the rankling grew stronger in his breast. He itched to pump lead into Jacob Fenwick; there had never been any-thing in his whole life he wished more to do; never.

So when word came (none remembered later who brought it), that the Old Man had been seen southeast along the ridges of his own country, it seemed more than likely, for once, that there might be truth to it. What stuck in Pete Bunsen's mind was the rumour had it, simply, that he'd been seen. Not lead-ing an army; not pouring down out of the hills with savages at his back. Not breathing fire and brimstone nor waving a clenched fist, but simply fading out over a landswell back in the scrub-oak country beyond the old stone house. A ghost returned to haunt with wring-ing sadness, the place where his sweat and toil had been spent. Where his seed had been planted; grown thick and mighty and faded away into nothing.

So Bunsen told no one where he was going,

not even the sad-faced dark woman with chil-
dren round her legs like puppies. He just
saddled up, weighted himself down with
armament and rode through the blood-red
sunlight of late afternoon, southeastward. A
few who saw him go, shrugged, spoke a little
among themselves. There would be no mourn-
ing if he never returned. Others, still with zeal
for the search, ran for their horses.

He rode slowly overland making no attempt
to conceal his coming until the slow dusk refused to shelter him, then he picked his way
over the lilting prairie and kept a screening of
trees, of sage and bluish chapparral between
him and the far country ahead.

By nightfall he was close to the stone house.
He'd been there many times since the fight;
since he'd watched the settlement men haul
back their wounded and slain in creaking wagons, slow as snails. He'd passed by often and
always the ugly stone house mocked him.
Now, sitting atop a low knoll among scrub-
oaks, peering down, he promised himself to
return one day with dynamite and demolish
Fenwick's Fort.

(He would never do it; the stone house
would stand for seventy years, crumbling,
mouldering, hushed and remembering, then
others would break it up, level the ground.
Fill the dug-well with stones in order to have

an uninterrupted sweep for tractors when they farmed the rich and dark-stained soil).

For Pete Bunsen there would be no future, with that stone-memory limned in his mind, stark-vivid and eternal, so he resolved to destroy it and while he looked downward at the squatness, the dark blockiness all splashed with moonglow and shadow, there was movement, swift and subtle. His hand closed hard around the reins while his heart pounded sturdily in its dark place. Movement . . .

He dismounted and hoped while fearing to hope. The old devil wouldn't be there. With all the back-country, he wouldn't be there; the one place associated with his memory in all men's minds.

Bunsen looped the reins and drew out his carbine from the saddleboot in a smooth motion, never taking his stare from the welter of soft, sad light down below. And he began to skirt around the slope, angling down it, holding to the shadowy places so moonlight wouldn't reflect off his gun barrel. Hoping harder than he'd ever hoped—slipping carefully along so that it took him a long lifetime to get close.

But the movement didn't come again and disappointment grew stronger as he crept forward. It could have been a hundred things. A skulking coyote drawn by the smell of rancid food, green-whiskered and rotting, inside. It could have been a famished hog from the old Parkinson place. Even an owl skimming past, or a varmint of some kind; a skunk, a 'possum, a 'coon. But it had been man-high, so hope fought with doubt as he made a wide circle, came down around the old barn slumbering in the moonlight, laid flat upon the ground and thrust his head around an edge of the building towards the house.

Nothing. There was only stillness as solemn as death, twice as lasting. He bit his lip and tugged at his beard with a hard crushing upon his spirit. God hear me; let him *be* here!

And he was.

The moon broke free from a cloud's opaque grasp and burnt down with silver glare upon a horse, tucked up, head-hung and drowsing, half hidden on the lee-side of the stone house. Bunsen saw it, fascinated, unable to look away from it, although for all he knew it might be a stray. But no—he *knew*. There was an answer to his pagan prayer across the milky yard and while he'd seen only the swish of that horse's tail from up on the knoll, it had been beckoning as surely as though God had beckoned Himself. Bunsen licked his lips until they shone with transparent spit. And eased the carbine forward through the dust, search-

221

ing for the bony old frame he longed to hear bullets smash into with their harsh and screaming fury.

The wait was long, the tension great, and when he thought he could bear it no longer, a shadow glided across the opening behind a broken door, dangling by one big wrought hinge. Bunsen went low behind his gun, drew it close with the wood indenting his cheek, waiting for a reappearance. When the shadow moved again he fired.

The broken door shuddered as though someone had flung out a hand to steady himself, but beyond the spanking echo, there was no sound at all.

Sweat burst out over Bunsen, made great dark arcs at the armpit, grew greasy along his twitching belly and over the hunch of his shoulders. The horse was looking towards the barn, its ears as straight as pointing fingers.

He'd killed him; he'd laid the Old Man low in the dinginess of the stone house. He was squirming in there bleating out his wretched soul. No. No; you couldn't count on a man dying from one bullet. Especially an old fiend like Jacob Fenwick. Be patient, he told himself. Be still as death and watchful, for the old devil will drag himself out to kill shortly, like a rattler with a broken back, swollen with venom and striking blind.

Time dragged. There was menace in each breath he sucked up. The Old Man was unhurt; he was slipping around phantom-like to get behind the barn. The vividness made Bunsen wince from an imaginary bullet and when he could stand it no longer, he called out.

"Fenwick! Fenwick, come out of there!"

Silence deeper than any he'd ever encountered closed down behind the words, gripped the yard in a hold of ice.

"Come out, you old devil. Your only chance's to come out and give up."

The answer came bold and loud, like iron striking an anvil. "I know who you are. Providence brought you here, Bunsen. Providence . . . I been stalking you for days, but you were scairt to leave the settlement. Now you're here . . . Yes; I'll come out, you black-hearted scoundrel. I'll come out."

But there was no movement by the broken door and Bunsen pressed lower against the earth with the hammer back on his carbine; with his lips sucked flat and his eyes slitted so tightly the lashes looked like ragged tree stubble. Waiting . . .

"Come on, Fenwick; I'm here. You wanted me here and I'm here. Come on."

"I'm coming," the Old Man called again, but still there was no movement and Bunsen

223

raised his head a mite, stared hard to see if there was movement any place at all, beyond the door, on either side of it. There wasn't.

He went down again, withdrawing his head like a turtle; grim, as tight inside as a coiled spring, and an idea began to form in his mind. The Old Man was too hard-hit to crawl out, or he was unarmed. He hadn't shot; for some reason he was unable to fight back. For some reason . . . Either because he was bad-hurt or something else, but whatever, the Old Man was helpless.

Muscles slackened in Bunsen's back. He rolled to one side and grew bold, raised his head. There was no shot. Hunched up his legs, drew up out of the weeds and peered over the lowest corral stringer. Still there was no sound, no movement, no shot.

"I'm coming after you, Fenwick. I'm coming in after you, you old devil. Say a prayer you doddamned murderer—I'm coming in after you."

The Old Man's voice was muffled when he replied. As though he was far off. "You scum—come on!"

The very faintness of the voice emboldened Bunsen. Like the Old Man was belly-down, face pressed flat upon the trodden floor, mouth muffled by dust and dirt clogging it.

Bunsen rose still higher, until he could see

over the next stringer. He was outlined then, a dusky shadow thick and black. No lance of flame leapt at him from the stone house, so he stood up full height in plain sight, holding his carbine across a pole, hugging it close. The silence grew thicker, oppressively heavy and deep. For some reason the Old Man wasn't going to fire. The thought returned that he was unarmed; that he was helpless to lift a gun.

Bunsen began to move, slowly at first, crouched and cautious. By the time he got to the end of the corral, he was upright, striding with a grim tread across the pale, glittering yard with moist moonlight like diluted milk around him, carbine held in both hands, low, steady as a rock.

Closer, he saw a bulky shape propped against thc front of the stone house. Sitting there like a man, legs thrust out along the ground, torso upright, leaning back. Something across the shadow's lap, vague and lost in shadow, looked dark and long; a rifle.

There was a slumpedness, a puffiness to the figure, but in Bunsen's wrought mind it was the Old Man and he fired into the shape and saw it twitch. Levered and fired again. Levered and hung a slippery finger upon the trigger, waiting. The dark object which had been across the lap lay aside in the dust. Silence . . .

225

Pete Bunsen gathered his weight and went forward, crooked finger taut upon the smooth fang of trigger, snout of his carbine looming, boring thirstily through the gloom until he was twenty feet away, fifteen feet, ten.

From his right came a single smashing roar. A great bursting glow of flame diminishing to a point. Echoes that chased each other up and out and down the night, louder by far than Bunsen's carbine had been, lingered.

Bunsen's arms flexed, flung forward. His gun hit the ground and exploded, the bullet crashing into the stone house at ground level. He staggered and hung his head until it seemed he couldn't remain upright, black beard low upon his chest, and the Old Man stalked him from around the corner of the house, rifle held up, club-like. A stringy, gaunt spectre with matted hair and cheeks so sunken the bones showed through. Deep-set eyes, white with madness, and saliva speckled with crusted dirt around his mouth.

Limping, dragging himself, but indomitable. Blind with a wildness that crashed cymbal-loud inside his head. Roared and drowned out all but the will to stumble a hundred yards and beat down the man in whose chest his last bullet had found lodging.

"Oh, you filth," the Old Man thundered, loud as Moses on The Hill. "You murdering black-hearted scum!"

He swung the empty musket, quivering muscles rigid with the violence which bore him up. Bunsen yawed wide when the blow descended, yawed and staggered, unheeding the splinter of bone when the stock crunched down.

The Old Man swung again and again and finally Bunsen toppled like a stricken tree. Fell full length face forward. Lay in the wet light while the Old Man swung the musket again and yet again, until exhaustion and a whirling before his eyes made him stagger, push the broken stock against the earth and lean upon it swallowing huge gulps of air.

Peter Bunsen was dead.

The Old Man breathed heavily, in and out, until a vestige of clarity returned. Then he used the shattered rifle to poke at Bunsen. Lift him up and flop him over upon his back like a wet sack, half full.

Moonlight reflected from the milky stare. Bunsen's beard was defiled with dust and saliva. It was shaggy, mussed and dull, and triumph twisted the Old Man's face as he gazed upon his fallen foe. A slow rhythm growing from the silence grew insistently louder. Beat up into a thudding that reverberated in the night. He stiffened off the broken musket, head canted as of old, listening, face growing crafty, sunken eyes agleam with stealth and wiliness; speckle-maned old wolf, all crippled and bruised from running, facing again the hunters who slavered for his blood.

The wave of sound grew, beating upon the night, then he saw them top out upon a spending hill that arose from the breast of the studded prairie beyond. Horsemen. Riders with a winkling of moonlight off their guns. In a moment of hesitancy they lingered in plain sight, then began the descent. Dust lifted, metallic scented, faint yet stirring like a miasma floating above a stinking sump.

He watched their course, calculated their numbers and threw down the useless rifle. Dragged himself by one good leg as rapidly as he was able, to the side of the horse which stood listening beside the stone house. Scrabbled at its mane, pulled himself upwards with a sour groan and dropped down. Remembering Bunsen's carbine when it was too late, he sawed the rope-rein in a frenzy as the riders came loping across the emptiness, a dark host of phantoms. Urged the horse out into the open with the one leg which still obeyed him and fled across the yard.

A great scream went up. Two dozen eyes caught movement at the same time, for there was no cover short of the barn. And it was ironic because the very man who fled now, had methodically destroyed all verdant life for a hundred yards around the stone house decades before. The shelter he'd deprived skulking Indians of, now left him naked to those who pursued him.

He rode wild and dishevelled, a scarecrow caricature on a worn-out horse, while deep within the shrunken spirit he knew the end was close, for his last bullet had killed Pete Bunsen. Defence lay in escape upon a stumbling horse, and so abrupt had been the emergence of his enemies he'd had neither time nor thought to take arms from the slain sheriff.

So the only hope lay in flight, and in that he was out-matched. *Their* horses were strong and eager. The nag he bestrode was sore and bony from too much riding, too little rest and provender. If escape lay within his ken, then it must come out of the secret knowledge he had of the land itself.

Those who pursued him came fast, their cries thin and lustful in the soft night. Several slid to a hard stop by Bunsen's body and their howls of horror rose stiff and clarion-like in the wake of those who raced past, panting after the Old Man.

A few fired pistols, but the range was great for short-guns and all knew rifle fire was too unsure from the pounding backs of horses, so they held their rifles high and used them as flails to urge onward the beasts they rode.

The Old Man made for the tangled growth and dark shadows of the upland where the hidden cave was and his horse laboured terribly up each hill. There was no doubt in his mind that if he got there safely, the horse was finished. It would never serve him again. Knowing, he used it cruelly, driving it blindly, seeking to wring the last leap from its faltering legs, its pumping lungs.

For a while he gained. That was because he knew the trails while the pursuit over-ran frequently, had to backtrack, find his sign before pushing on again. His imperious will and doughty craft kept him well ahead the first hour. After that, fierce hope dwindled. The horse was going up and down, but failed to cover much ground, its legs working mechanically, by instinct, its mind blanked over with red froth to match the fluted opening of roaring nostrils. The Old Man clubbed the animal with his fist, but it could go no faster, no further.

When it collapsed he sprang cat-like, long arms clawing wide, and lit upright. The nearest pursuers were crashing through the brush close behind. He heard them swearing excitedly, yelling to one another, flung himself at the sage, burrowing into it with a great threshing, mouth wide for air, face torn and bleeding, clothing shredded by the spines. Then he heard their mingling howls to one another when they came upon his dying horse. Yells of triumph that went bouncing off across the broken land.

He scrabbled through the brush in a frantic effort to stave off the inevitable. At his hip a sheath-knife caught often and had to be extricated. He closed his eyes and plunged straight into the densest tangle, ignoring sharp little spikes which tore into his flesh, until it was slippery with blood.

Came at last, weaving, lungs afire, wounded leg as numb as stone, to a drop-off lip of shale and across the way he could see dark shadows pressed flat against a granite upthrust where the cave was.

And that instant a rifle exploded. Over its reverberations a man screamed exultantly. "I see him! Yonder, at the edge of the brush!"

The Old Man was twisting, bending forward to lose himself in spiny covert when the second shot came searing low through the brush, its passage marked with a whipping and a snarl and his breath was forced out when it struck him with a loud, wet sound. A thick, sodden echo danced briefly over his frame and died. He fell, but sage held him up, sagging and all but spent. Hurt and numb, so that his lower body wouldn't respond to his will, but more exhausted than in pain.

They came cursing through the brush, beating it down, trampling what they forced past, clubbing limbs aside with musket butts and panting so hard the Old Man heard them sixty seconds before the first one gave a throaty call; before he saw the looming shadow of a destroyer slide across the ground in front of his eyes and heard the rattling pull of the man's breathing.

And thought in detachment of how his wife had drawn the bucket up from the dug-well, filled and slopping with cool, clear water.

"I got him!"

The shout triggered some unknown reservoir of energy, of mad desperation. Feeling returned to the worn-out body, energy gushed for the last time through the shrivelled veins and the Old Man flung up off the brush and drew his sheath-knife. Threw himself upon the astonished man, whose face blanched white as he stumbled, flung up his pistol-arm to protect himself from the blur of steel.

"Shoot him! One o' you *shoot him!"*

A roar thundered past the Old Man's lips, gaping wide, pink with froth. The posseman tumbled backwards into the sage and the blade whooshed past his throat by inches. He scrambled with a wildness to get clear as others

232

plunged up and one man, squat, dark, with a boulder-like body, planted himself before the Old Man, pistol raised and cocked.

"Stop Fenwick!"

The Old Man was deaf. He hurled himself deeper into the constricting sage towards the squat man, who leapt quickly away. Then they were all around him, guns up, but fearful lest they hit one another. The squat man circled, pistol still up, his weight forcing the sage to give way. The Old Man swung blindly at them where they stood with brutal mouths twisted from running and the squat man got his chance; flung himself upon the Old Man from the rear. His hand-gun made a vicious short arc. There was a thud and the Old Man staggered, half lowered his arm and let off a great pealing roar. Again, again, the pistol crunched down. Finally, the Old Man fell, hung in the sage of a soggy heap.

"Holy Mother," a man said in awe. "I never seen the likes."

"Get him out of here. Come on, take an arm."

The squat man got under the staggered inert form, began to struggle back out of the thicket with it. Others helped, some just trudged along in the strange and terrible silence staring hollow-eyed at the wasted, ragged scarecrow which had been Old Man Fenwick.

233

They took him back to the stone house and put him on the ground, not far from Pete Bunsen's corpse. He shuddered and groaned. They stood around, buzzards waiting for the cow to die. The squat man went to his saddle, took down the rope that hung there and bent his head so that shadows hid his face; began to fashion a hangman's noose.

Someone said, "You was against hangin' the other one—how come you'll hang this one?"

"The difference is," the squat man said, "the boy's not a killer. Not a cold-blooded killer. But for the Old Man he wouldn't be standin' on the brink right now. But this— that one there—he's a devil an' got no right to live."

A grizzled man with a tarnished silver star upon his hip-holster stared stonily at the Old Man. "He's plumb crazy, this old devil. I got no great likin' for killing, but I'll be proud to yank the rope that strangles the Old Man."

There was an austere-faced man kneeling at the Old Man's side. From the ground he said, "It won't make much difference whether we lynch him or not."

"Why?"

The kneeling man rocked back. "He's dying. Look here: in one of his brushes with a posse he's been hard-hit in the right leg. It's all green with infection. All supperating. That shot up on the ridge—here—beside his spine and out the front."

The kneeling man got up, pocketed his hands. "In fact, boys," he concluded, "if we don't work fast, we'll be stringing up a dead man."

They hung the Old Man to a baulk of his own barn within plain sight of his stone house, built a little fire over by the dug-well and hunkered there waiting out the hours, speaking little, rarely glancing at the gently spiralling figure, drawn out long and lean, twisting softly from a length of rope.

The range grew peacefully quiet, as though surcease had come at last. The little fire dwindled. Grave men, weary and a-sprawl, gazed into it. Stars glittered in the might sweep of heaven, cold, distant, and countless.

The austere man arose finally. "All right," he said, "let's be getting back."

They took the Old Man down, tied him across a horse and started for the settlement, each with thoughts hidden by night-shadows and low-tugged hatbrims and when they went with muffled slowness over the dusty roadway to Osage, dawn was showing blood-red off in the west.

Pete Bunsen was buried in the little cemetery with the slatfence to keep animals out;

not far from the grave of preacher Harry Cumberland and several other new mounds.

The Old Man's face was washed. He was covered, all but that much, with an Army blanket and laid out upon a billiard table for all to see. Captain Wilson ordered it thus, his reason simply that, while he'd had no hand in the apprehension, the People of Indian Territory, notoriously lawless, should take a long look and remember the inevitability of retribution, whether by the Army or by their fellows.

Of punishment for the lynching, nothing was said. In fact, no inquiry was made at all. Captain Wilson brushed his moustache upwards with eyes a-glitter and thought, if they would hang enough of each other, the Army wouldn't have to go riding sixty miles on a handful of hardtack to do it for them—Secesh scum.

Matthew heard it from a jailer and doubted, so the man brought him a lock of the speckled mane. He called up the short corridor to Carl and told him of the Old Man's end. His brother's silence was answer enough.

Several days went by. There was a creeping bite to the wind that sucked around buildings. A restlessness among the people. Captain Wilson sat long hours in the improvised courtroom listening to the defences of those being tried for attacking United States soldiers; meted out justice in accordance with the times, his own asperity of disposition, and behind him were one hundred and seventy bayonets which precluded riot, or even complaint, for the settlement was glutted with killings, was exhausted from the constant riding, longed only to have done with it and return to its pretty jealousies, its avid suspicions and its endless gossip.

When the last trail was over, the last miscreant against Justice—which was Marital Law—drew his sentence and was led away and the courtroom was cleared, Captain Wilson looked down where Sergeant Dennis hunched over a tiny table cluttered with papers, and asked for the next case.

Dennis said, "We're done with these, sir. There's just them's still in the jailhouse."

"Then let's take them in order of importance and have done with it. Which name is next?"

"It's put down here in the order they was taken. The next one's Matthew Fenwick."

"Guard! Bring the accused over."

They brought Matthew across the roadway heavy with chains. He wore a soldier's shirt, which did nothing to leaven the rancour felt by the settlement folk who watched him being led past. His trousers had also been replaced by the largest pair that could be found. They left inches of ankle showing and flapped grotesquely when he walked. His face was still purple with scabs while his thick auburn thatch, hurriedly combed, was a-tumble in the breeze.

Captain Wilson looked upon the giant with a jaundiced eye. Except for Matthew, his soldiers wouldn't have been mauled. So far he'd made no report of the riot, but he'd have to eventually, he'd have to, and who knew better than a career soldier how those things were interpreted, written into a man's service record, emerged to haunt and accuse him when he sought promotions.

"The oath, Sergeant."

It was given and Matthew mumbled, inclined his head. Sergeant Dennis resumed his seat, held his pen poised.

"This is a Military Court," Captain Wilson said by rote, without intonation, gazing out at the silent spectators on benches, seeing their locked expressions of antipathy and letting words roll on, a preamble considered necessary in order that the accused might understand what was to come, what he might expect. When he finished, Wilson's gaze moved to Matthew, lingered there a moment while the hush deepened and Dennis' pen dipped, ran frantically over the paper.

"Matthew Fenwick, you are charged with destruction of property, theft, with attempted murder and murder. How do you plead?"

Matthew was rooted, torn within and unable to answer.

Captain Wilson waited, his most crushing stare bent upon the accused. "Can there be doubt in your mind, Mr. Fenwick? Your hands are stained red. The bruises I see, came to be where they are because of the indignation of the people. Do you believe so many citizens could be wrong in their estimation of you—and those others who were with you?"

"Sir; my brother—"

"It is not your brother who is being tried here, Mr. Fenwick. It is you and you alone. Except insofar as your brother was a participant in your crimes, mentioning him will not aid you."

Matthew looked steadily into the cold face; read his sentence there as clearly as though it were printed in black letters. In his mind a voice sounded, booming loud, but distant, as though crying down the years, or from some distant place. *You will survive!*

"The court waits, Mr. Fenwick."

Dark waters flooded his soul. It was a dream, standing there on trial for his life. Knowing what the outcome must be. Hearing the Old Man's voice so clear above lesser noises—sounds of the settlement beyond the walls, the barking of dogs, the rasp of men coughing, spitting, calling to one another out where the autumnal sun rode high and pleasant with streamers of breeze to cool it. Looking down into upturned faces, all closed against him and satisfied with the knowledge how this must end.

"Answer!"

He swallowed without saliva. A hotness, a dryness, made the words husky, when at last they came. "I'm guilty. I'm guilty against my will, but I'm guilty."

Captain Wilson looked at the sergeant. "He pleads guilty. That's all you need write. In fact, sergeant, the way this is going and because you're already behind with your transcripts, just put down what is essential, what is *meant,* in as few words as possible, not particularly what is *said.*"

"Yes, sir."

"Now, Mr. Fenwick—fourteen days ago today, did you go with your father and several others to the home of a woman named Harris and participate in the murder there, of a man named Harry Cumberland?"

"I was there."

"Yes or no. Just answer my questions yes or no."

" . . . Yes."

240

"And again, did you participate in the murder of a man named Will Parson?"

"No!"

"Do you know how he was killed or by whom?"

"No!"

"All right. Now then; did you deliberately and in cold blood shoot down a man in the livery stable of Osage settlement, named Joshua Thompson?"

"No; I shot at no man in the livery barn. Do you mean when we were escaping from the Osage jailhouse?"

"Yes."

"No, sir. That was my father. I was behind him and John Parkinson was in front of me. I could see both of them and it was the Old Man fired at the hostler — or whoever he was."

"Did you shoot at anyone at all, during your fight here in Osage?"

"I . . . Yes, I did. I shot at a man behind a curtain across the road from the jailhouse. I couldn't see him, but he threshed around after I fired and he didn't shoot any more."

"Is that the only person you fired at?"

Matthew's gaze grew misty. "I've got no clear memory of that fight," he said. "I've tried to remember. If I could, I'd tell you."

Tiredly, Captain Wilson said, "There is no need."

It had the ring of doom to it, that weary voice. A sound of coldness, almost disinterest, as though Wilson had all he wanted—which he *did* have. It was there, spinning out darkly from the tip of Sergeant Dennis' pen, cramped and hardly legible, but there . . . Yes, I was there when the Old Man killed Cumberland. Yes, I stole horses to flee upon. Yes, I shot a man behind a curtain. I am a killer. I am a horsethief, which is punishable by death in Neutral Ground, as elsewhere in the West, where men's lives depend upon fleetness, the handiness of their mounts.

The people upon the benches began to jostle, to become restless. They had sat through many trials by now and they *knew*.

Matthew didn't think the fight against his life had hardly begun, but *he* hadn't seen the other trials; he didn't *know*. He watched Captain Wilson, who leaned upon the table, long booted legs thrust out under it, hands clasped bonily together, pale where they rested beneath his chin, apparently thinking, with hooded eyes partially closed, for all the world like a sun-washed serpent upon a rock, all peaceful and quiet, but with a beating heart ready upon an instant's notice to rouse up and lash out.

"Sir," Matthew said.

242

Wilson bristled, face swelling with irritation at the interruption. "Quiet. You speak here only when you're spoken to."

The silence thickened, drew down over the room so that each pair of ears heard the slightest sound, the gentlest rustle of clothing, smothered clearing of a throat. Until at last, Captain Wilson learned back in his chair and gazed at the sergeant.

"Caught up?"

The sergeant, still scribbling, nodded, and Wilson bent his gaze to Matthew.

In that horrifying instant, Matthew's hope departed forever and he understood that Wilson hadn't been thinking; hadn't been deliberating his fate; had simply been killing time until the sergeant had all the trial's transcript brought up to the moment of sentencing. It was shattering and it was true. He read it in the thin face across from him. His trial was over. There hadn't been a witness called, an argument in his favour of any kind. No defence, no offence, just the stated charges and his answers.

He didn't know what extenuating circumstances were, but neither did others in that room. However, he *felt* them; felt he should have the right to explain why he had been in Widow Harris' house—why he had taken horses—how he had struggled to bring the

243

Old Man to reason.

"Mr. Fenwick." It was as though Wilson had read his mind. As though the force of his own thoughts had been impelled across the room by desperation; the things which were crying inside him to be heard.

"Mr. Fenwick. If Justice requires that your life be taken for the crimes you have told us you committed, I want you to know that such a verdict is arrived at through logic, through careful consideration, and through compassion. Have you anything to say before I give the verdict?"

He started to lift his hands. The weight of chains held them down. "I—did what was done because I had to. I didn't fight to kill folks, I fought to survive. I been taught to do that since I was big enough to pack a gun. Me and my brother both."

"Were you also taught to steal horses?"

It was hopeless, futile. He sagged, the weight of manacles dragging at him. "Unless I took those horses, sir, they'd have caught and killed me."

"But nevertheless, you stole them; you broke the law and you killed people while outside the law."

Matthew stood mute, a great powerful man without words, without any knowledge, save that which told him he was facing death.

Captain Wilson thumped the table; words flowed from him without inflection, without pause or lapse, so that they ran together, a blur of sound spoken from memory:

"This court finds you guilty of theft of attempted murder and of murder and if it errs may our Maker pardon it for seeing justice and truth in what it does. Court dismissed."

Wilson leaned back with a nod to Matthew's guards. "Date of execution tomorrow morning at ten sharp. Take him back . . . Any questions, Sergeant?"

"No, sir."

He was put in with Carl, away from Ellie and Judith Anne. There was a coldness in him, a drugged feeling of lassitude. It was hard for him to look into his brother's face, for there were worse bruises there than upon his own features. The day of the riot, Carl had been unmercifully beaten by a jailer, too fearful of entering the real battle, but who beat Carl with a length of chain when the younger son had cried out through the slotted window. Now, the purple wreckage was more than he could stand, so he dropped down upon a pallet and smelt Fall coming through the little window overhead.

"Did they try you, Matthew?"

"Yes; I was tried."

Carl edged closer, knelt with fear bright in

245

his eyes. "Did that soldier give a verdict? What did he say . . . ?"

How to tell the truth and stand the anguish, the howls which would follow, until the jailer came? How to explain that within, a dark seed was blossoming, giant obsidian petals soft and warm, were curling about his spirit in which defeat had lain since he had surrendered— and even before?

There was no way. There had been enough suffering; more than enough. There wasn't a living person close by who wouldn't bear scars upon his soul for years to come, from all this. Not one. Not among the soldiers or among the settlement folk, or even among those who, travelling through, had camped a while nearby. They would each remember . . . Why? Because the Old Man had made it so, that was why. The Old Man and his strangeness.

He knotted his fists and held them tightly against his body. Kid Marcy, so dim in memory now, had said it wasn't important, not really; that you were here, in time, in space, coming from mystery and darkness, touching bright sunlight only briefly, then moving on into blackness and mystery again. He was right.

"What did he *say*, Matthew?"

"I'm to go back tomorrow morning . . . at ten o'clock."

A small lie; more a deceit than a lie. Without moving his eyes from the ceiling where flyspecks lay in thick disarray, he saw Carl push upright and walk towards the slotted windows. Knew he was peering out, smelling Fall, loving it as Matthew loved it, with a moment's respite in his head because Matthew had deceived him.

It was impossible for Matthew to rest, although he tried, and after nightfall, he kept Carl in conversation, speaking swiftly and softly and low, memory largely in each word, reliving it. Memory and pain that he struggled to hide, until Carl wilted with weariness. Then he talked harder, and even once put his hand upon his brother's shoulder and let it lie there, feeling the great curve of muscle while he groped for something which eluded him; something which would hold back time so that they might re-live their lives step by step, day by day, all over again in the darkness.

When dawn came, Carl was sprawled in troubled slumber upon his pallet and Matthew stood by the window watching the streaks turn from grey to mauve to pearl to palest pink, and finally to the gentlest of blues, with a hint of red, which was daylight.

Osage stirred. It was uncanny how clear and sharp every detail of life was now. He saw

247

a hostler down by the livery stable come out into the new day and welcome it with a great spray of dark brown spittle. Watched him scan the sky, tongue his cud deeper into his pouched cheek, turn and disappear, dragging a long-handled manure fork behind him.

Later, when slab-sided dogs were sniffing along the roadway hopefully, and people were moving about, an open wagon left the livery barn with a team of satiny bay horses. He admired them, the way the sun shone from their curried hides, until they went past and he saw the pine box rattling in the wagon-bed.

The hardest thing of all was to eat. Carl was full of hope and advice and plied him with things he must tell the soldiers, while they squatted like caged animals over dented tins of greasy food. Stew clung to the roof of his mouth, clogged his throat and refused to be swallowed. Later, when the sun was ten o'clock high, he heard them coming for him. He stood up at the dull clomp of their boots.

"I prayed yesterday," his brother said. "I'll pray twice as hard today. Remember; there's ain't a man that's got no right to fight for his life, Matthew."

"You pray," Matthew said, and took his brother's hand and held it in both of his. "And, something else . . ."

"What?"

248

"Ellie."

Carl's face burnt red. "I wanted to tell you, but it was hard, Matthew."

"That's all right, Carl. She was good for you."

"She's with child, Matthew."

"I reckon so," Matthew said. "It would work out like that with the two of you. I'm glad, Carl."

"Fenwick; let's go!"

Carl's big hand dropped as Matthew started towards the swinging door. "You tell them, Matthew. I'll pray. I'll call down for Ellie to pray."

"Do that, Carl. Good-bye. Tell Ellie good-bye for me."

He moved swiftly, hurrying, big legs like pistons, pumping, rising and falling, going past the cell where the girls were without looking around, for he couldn't see very well, things swam.

He heard Ellie call his name, softly, like music. Heard, but dared not turn and when he got to the end of the corridor, there were others to take him through the office and out-side and down the plankwalk where soldiers stood guard at spaced intervals, bayonets on their muskets.

The gibbet was behind town. It struck him as decent it should be there, out of sight sort of. When he first saw it there was a tightening behind his belt for it stood clear against the morning sky. Tall, upright and stark, with new rope as thick as a man's wrist, dangling yellowly, straight and still, for now there wasn't a trace of the breeze.

And all around it were soldiers in lines, their backs to the scaffold, sunlight shinning off their bayonets. Captain Wilson was on the platform, watching Matthew come up with his guard. Matthew could see the still intentness on Wilson's face; held his gaze rock-like and returned the Captain's regard stare for stare. Then Wilson stirred, cast a look at two pale-faced soldiers with drawn sabers standing near two small chocks with a smaller piece of rope between them.

He descended the steps with one hand holding his sword by the hilt so that it wouldn't strike, and he stopped before the guard, nodded to the sergeant, who dismissed them. There was transparent perspiration across the sergeant's face and if there was any compassion anywhere, that sparkling morning, it was in that one face.

"We have a preacher here, Mr. Fenwick," Captain Wilson said. "You are allowed five minutes to pray."

Now that there was no longer the faintest doubt, the smallest hope, he wanted to have it

250

over with, so he shook his head.

"Then you can use the time talking, if you wish."

To Matthew's mind that was equally futile. He reached out with his chained hands and touched a dark hood which hung from Wilson's hands. "Do I have to wear that?"

"No, you don't *have* to. It is so you won't see them cut the rope which springs the trap and so your face will be hidden afterwards, but you aren't compelled to wear it."

"Who's to see me afterwards?"

"Well . . ."

"Will you cut me down and put me on a slab for the settlement folks to see?"

"It's usually done that way, yes."

"Then let me use my last five minutes asking you not to. Those people aren't my friends. Can't you cut me down and just bury me?"

Captain Wilson gazed into the clear eyes and nodded. "If that's your wish, yes, I can do it."

"Thank you."

They turned him, steered him along by the elbows and mounted the steps on either side of him. It didn't seem that he was walking into Eternity, simply that he was climbing steps. Like the rickety ones at the Parkinson place, which was built on logs up off the

251

ground. Like any plank steps. It was the brush of rope across his cheek which fetched him up. He moved away from it and at his feet was the outline of a trapdoor. He moved off a little from that, too. Turned and looked out.

As far as he could see was a clearness. A brilliance which only Fall brought. An un-hampered freeness of air, of sky and earth. Eastward where the places he knew, had known since childhood. Chagrin Creek, Parkinson's place ... names, memories, thoughts and recollections as bright as the day itself.

"We'll bind your arms now."

They did; tightly to his sides. His ankles, too, so that he had trouble standing upright, had to be placed upon the little trapdoor by soldiers who got red-faced from straining at his great weight. Captain Wilson was sweat-ing. His handsome moustache lent breadth to an otherwise shallow facial structure, which at this moment, was nearly white.

When he straightened up from supervising the placing of Matthew upon the trapdoor, he still held the black hood. "If you'll look straight ahead," he said, "you'll never know. Maybe you'd prefer this after all?"

"No, I won't need that. Captain; I know it's your duty to do this. I ain't mad or vengeful towards you."

"Thank you, Fenwick."

"Please tell my brother why I didn't tell him I was being hung this morning, will you?"

Wilson blinked.

"He's suffered so much; not just lately, but always. He was always the gentlest of the family. He never hurt a human bein' in his life. I just couldn't tell him last night."

"I understand. I'll tell him. God rest you . . . I'm sorry; truly sorry."

The signal was when Captain Wilson stepped back. For seconds it seemed to the men with drawn sabers that he never would. Then he moved. Instantly both sabers swung mightily the rope between the chocks was severed. The trap crashed open, rope spun out, jerked with a quivering they could feel through their boot-soles, then began to swirl gently round and round.

"Lay him out, Captain?"

"No. Did they finish the grave?"

"Yes, sir."

"Then please take him there and bury him."

Sergeant Dennis looked up sharply. He had served under this thin officer for three years and it was the first time he'd ever heard him say please to an enlisted man.

"Yes, sir."

"Sergeant . . ."

"Sir?"

"I wish it was possible to know how a man was going to die before he was hung."

Dennis looked down. "It's better we don't know, sir," he said. "Much better."

Wilson stood back while they put Matthew on the shutter and, with a soldier at each end and one on each side, bore him away. Now he was clay. The Army blanket covered all of him except his lower legs and booted feet, which hung down and dangled.

"He was a big man, Sergeant."

"Yes, sir. You want that preacher taken over there before they cover him up?"

"He didn't seem to want that."

"Ah, but he should have, Captain, he should have." It appalled Sergeant Dennis' Catholic sensibilities, thinking of a man going off without prayer.

"All right; but tell him only to say that a brave man lies in the box. Never mind the forgiveness-for-crimes part of it."

As Dennis moved off, an enlisted man came up with a salute. "Sir; the settlement folks have appointed a new sheriff. He wants to know when you'll try the other Fenwick and them girls so he can have a clear jailhouse."

254

"Does he?" Wilson said, still and grave looking with sunlight burnishing his moustache. "Tell him in my own words, soldier, that the army'll clear his jailhouse for him when it's damned good and ready."

He went back to the shade of the courtroom, sat down behind the table and fingered idly through the mound of transcripts. People, lives, tribulations, they were all there. When he closed his eyes the face of Matthew was there, sightless, mouth closed without pressure. There was no pallor of death for the rope had ruptured a blood vessel and the ruddiness of life remained. When he opened his eyes to stare at the opening door an hour later, Sergeant Dennis was filling the opening, burly, thick, and faintly damp looking.

"All finished, Sergeant?"

"All done, sir."

"The prayer?"

"Like you said."

"All right. I guess we might as well have his brother brought over. We can hold three more trials and get out of this stinking hold if we hurry."

"Yes, sir."

"Sergeant . . . That girl, the long-legged one; what's she charged with?"

"Conspiracy, aiding the others, horse stealing, bein' an accessory to the Cumberland murder."

"That much, eh? Well; bring her over first."

When Judith Anne came, manacled, impassive, dark eyes sombre and unblinking, there was fatalism as thick as night in her expression. Captain Wilson gazed upon her, while the courtroom began to fill, people shuffled in as though a messenger had gone among them carrying the news of this girl's trial. He knew how the faces would be, pushed up sharply with curiosity, with antagonism, and refused to look over at them. Sergeant Dennis took his seat, held the pen up as though signalling he was ready.

"Your name?"

"Judith Anne Parkinson."

Questions, answers, pauses, the sound of chains, of people spitting surreptitiously upon the floor or blowing their noses with great explosive effort, or mumbling to one another. Sounds that droned, off-key, strident, or soft and muted, but sounds.

" . . . Did you *ever* fire the gun?"

"No."

"Not even for food?"

"No. Ask those who've got it now if it's been shot."

"I'm asking you!"

256

"I never shot it, no . . . sir."

"And you didn't get off your horse at the Harris Place? Didn't know why the Old Man and his son Matthew went inside?"

"Dennis' scratching pen, busy, lifting to pause then plummeting down again like a bird after an insect, striding with nervous haste over pages of paper while beaded sweat stood out upon the sergeant's face and his mouth was compressed with concentration.

With a tone of finality the verdict: " . . . Find you not guilty of conspiracy grand theft accessory to murder and if it errs may our Maker pardon it for seeing justice and truth in what it does court dismissed.

"Sergeant; have the other girl brought over quickly."

"Yes, sir."

Time to glance at his golden watch; a hard thought that time meant nothing here in this barbaric place except that the sun would set and rise, over and over again. That beauty of countryside would be turned on and off by an unknown hand and the people would scarcely look up except to sniff for rain, dumb to the eternal puzzle of—why?

"Your name."

"Ellie Parkinson."

"The charges against you . . . "

Oh—but this one was different. Still, with

a great abundance that would tighten the throat of any man. A bursting ripeness that was strength as well as beauty. His tiredness turned to gall. This was the kind, 'breed or not, to fill up a man. To make him feel mean when he touched her. It was there in her eyes. Her steady, hushed dark eyes.

" . . . So you fled with Carl Fenwick after the fight at the stone house and never saw the others again; had no part in any of the other fights."

"No."

This kind a man could mould his life around. This kind a man could seek and never find. Oh, God, I'm sick of this. I could heave, I'm so sick of it.

" . . . Not guilty court dismissed Sergeant have the man Carl Fenwick brought over."

"Sir?"

She hadn't moved. The lashes over her eyes shielded some strange, undefinable expression. He leaned upon the table.

"Yes; what is it, Miss Parkinson?"

"Carl . . ."

"What about him?"

"Sir—he knows. People came to his window and told him about his brother."

"*Who* went to his window?" Wrath erupted, ran like syrup inside his tried head. "Who— I want to know who. Sergeant! Goddamn it, I want the people who couldn't wait."

"Yes, sir."

"Now then—"

"He's not himself, sir. If you bring him to be tried he won't be himself. I want to ask you not to do it. Not to disgrace him. I want to beg that of you, Captain."

"Sit down. Guards—clear the room. Yes, everyone . . . Mister, I don't care who you are, I want this court cleared. Miss Parkinson . . . By God, sir, if I have to tell you again I'll have you tried for contempt! *Now get out!* All of you *get out!*"

Panting, fingers balled into fists and red behind the eyes, aching, tired eyes, he leaned over the desk stiff and ugly.

"Now; I want you to tell me how you came to be in that stone house. How you came to be mixed up in this mess at all. Your father didn't make you go into that house; he didn't force you to fight because you aren't the type to be coerced—then why?"

"Because of Carl."

"Oh. You're in love with him?"

"Yes." The dark eyes never wavered and the rich glow of health shone out at him, who was sallow and thin. "I'm with his child."

Wilson sat down. "I see. You're his wife."

"No; we aren't married. I was to meet him in the settlement the day Sheriff Bunsen put

259

them all in jail."

"You would have been married then?"

"I don't know. We hadn't talked of marriage."

"What were your plans after you met him here in the settlement, then?"

"Go away together. Go far away. We talked of a house somewhere. By a creek."

"Together?"

"Yes. But it's hard for others to understand. His paw had a hold on him. On him and Matthew both, but Matthew was more like the Old Man—up to the last time I saw him anyway. Carl never was like the Old Man, but he still had this hold on him. On all of them."

"There's something I remember from other testimonies; didn't you aid them in escaping from jail? Didn't you steal some horses for them to ride away on?"

Ellie nodded. "I did. I never denied it. If you'd asked me during my trial I'd have told you so."

"How do you justify breaking the law?"

"Justify it? Because I *knew* they hadn't killed Parson—that's how. I know the settlement people hated Fenwicks—and Parkinsons, too. It was wrong, what I did. I knew that when I stole the horses. If it hadn't been the settlement folks would have hung them I wouldn't have done it."

"So you broke the law to prevent a greater crime from being committed."

"Yes."

"That's how it'll go into my report anyway," Wilson said, and rapped the table with his knuckles. "If Carl Fenwick is released what will you do?"

"We'll go away. As far as we can get."

"And your sister?"

Ellie's face lengthened. "I don't know. Carl and I will go away alone—just us two."

"I can imagine." He gazed steadily at her. It was restful to see such beauty and the tension within him lessened. "But," and he arose, "I can't grant your request that Fenwick be allowed a delay."

She arose also. "Sir . . . ?"

"He's got to be tried."

"But tomorrow . . ."

"No, not tomorrow, today; now."

Her face crumpled, great dark eyes withdrawing from him, growing ugly with stoicism. The transformation held him. It was as though another girl, purely Indian, had slipped into her place.

Quietly he said, "I'm sorry."

" . . . To humble him. To bring him here like he is for settlement people to see."

"No, but because the Army's been here too long already. The Old Man is dead. Matthew
261

Fenwick is dead—executed. Those who interfered with the troops have been punished. Lady, the Army can't stay here forever."

"There's been enough unfairness, enough suffering."

He drew up straighter, gazing at her. "Come on; I'll take you back," and walked beside her to the door, past the sentinel there, down into the dusty roadway and across it where other soldiers patrolled. Stopped at the jailhouse as the sergeant came up, herding three raffish individuals, and called out to him.

"I got three of them, sir."

"These?" He looked coldly upon the shrinking men.

"Yes, sir."

"Take them out to dig holes, Sergeant. Long, deep holes."

"Holes? Where, sir?"

"Anywhere. Dig holes the rest of the day. When they get a lot of holes dug stand by and make them fill them up again. Do you understand?"

"I understand, sir."

"On second thought, detail it to some of the men who were hurt during the riot and you come with me."

He waited outside the jailhouse with Ellie beside him until the sergeant returned, then all three of them went inside.

Osage's new sheriff was a pompous man, fat without being big. He had none of Bunsen's coiledness, but there was animosity in his face.

"How is your prisoner, Fenwick?"

"Quiet now. All huddled in a corner and quiet."

"Get an escort, Sergeant. Bring him over to the courtroom."

"Cap'n; what about these ladies?"

"They're free."

"You mean turn 'em out?"

"Yes."

"I won't be responsible, Cap'n. There's considerable feeling."

Wilson turned back from the doorway. "*I'll* be responsible," he said. "I'll be a hundred and seventy bayonets responsible. Turn them out. The first person who molests them will have a long, long time to repent it."

He re-crossed the roadway, saw the veiled, slanted looks directed his way and was accosted by an unshaven, furtive man. "Captain; I got their team an' wagon."

"Whose team and wagon?"

"Fenwicks. When they come to Osage that first time."

"Oh; you mean you took it after they broke out of jail?"

"Yeh. You see—"

"Soldier! Do you know where the working detail is digging holes?"

"Yes, sir."

"Escort this man out there. He's to dig *twice* as many holes as the others. My orders, soldier."

"Yes, sir. Come along, you."

When Carl came there was a puffiness to his dark-ringed eyes, a slackness to his face. He moved as though incapable of seeing far ahead, in a groping way and Captain Wilson had no stomach for it. When the settlement people began shuffling in, buzzards flapping to the feast, he ordered the room cleared. Trumpeted it loud enough to be heard across the road.

Harrassed Sergeant Dennis shouldered through the retreating mob urgently. Went to his little table and took up the pen without glancing over at the shaggy giant who sat slumped, ox-like, across the room.

"Your name."

Silence.

"Your name!"

Carl raised his head and Captain Wilson, who had seen men's souls naked before, dropped his gaze to the mound of papers before him.

"There is no case here, Sergeant. He was

264

not with the others. He was in the stone-house-fight only, and as he has been said before, the attackers in that instance had no right at all on their side.

"Fill it in 'not guilty.' Sergeant; take him out. Have their wagon and team hunted up, brought to the jailhouse. He and the younger girl can trail with us as far as Hatchersville. That's not a very long way, but it's a start."

"Yes, sir."

THE END

We hope that you have enjoyed
reading this Chivers Large Print Book.
We publish more than 200 new
Large Print titles every year
and maintain an extensive backlist
of titles in nearly every genre.
For more information on other titles
or to receive a complete title list,
please call or write to us
at the address below—
we would love to hear from you!

Chivers North America
1 Lafayette Road
Post Office Box 1450
Hampton, New Hampshire 03842-0015
(800) 621-0182
(603) 926-8744